Truth and Beauty
(His Majesty's Theatre Book 3)

Christina Britton Conroy

Enjoy!

C.B.C

8/20

First published by Endeavour Press Ltd in 2017.

Table of Contents

Chapter One

Elly Fielding's terrified scream echoed down the narrow alley. A foul smelling cloth smothered her face. The chloroform was strong. She was unconscious in a second. Mick, the butcher's assistant, hoisted her over his shoulder and ran. Jake, the gallery worker, stuck a cork into the chloroform bottle, pulled off his loose yellow wig, and chased Mick around the corner to a covered farm cart. The street was deserted. He prayed no one had heard the scream.

Two huge horses shook their harnesses and snorted white mists into the freezing morning air. The shivering driver pulled his scarf half-way over his face, and watched Jake open the heavy back flap. He laughed as Mick tossed Elly inside, like a side of pork. She landed shoulder first on hard wood.

The excruciating pain woke Elly from her drugged sleep. Her pounding head felt huge and her eyes refused to focus. Bile flooded her mouth. She spit out bitter liquid as her empty stomach heaved, cramping painfully against itself.

Jake shouted to the driver, "Get going, Gus!"

Gus cracked his whip, and Elly felt the cart lurch. The horses' hooves fell into a graceful, hypnotic pattern. She surrendered to the strong opiate, closed her eyes, and sank into a deep sleep.

*

Jake and Mick rocked with the wagon's swaying motion. Crouched on filthy floorboards, they braced themselves against the taut canvas cover. Their breathing slowed as their eyes adjusted to the dark.

Mick chuckled. "We done it, just like you said. It were easy."

Jake clutched the bottle of chloroform between his legs. "We're far from 'done.' Today was easy, but I spent two days slaving in that stinking art gallery. At least we've got the girl. When we get her father's money, then we'll be done."

He held his nose with his left hand. With his right hand, he carefully peeled off hard glue around the edges. His skin stung, as he slowly pulled off a hard-rubber nose. He used a fingernail to scrape off the last of the dried paste. "God, I hate this thing." He started to toss the nose from the wagon, remembered that he might need it again, and tucked it into his pocket.

"You know, Mick, for almost two weeks I've been walking right past coppers. Stupid buggers! They're all on the lookout for Tommy Quinn and not a one noticed me."

Chapter Two

Town of Settle in Yorkshire, England, January 5, 1904

In frigid dawn air, investigative reporter Sam Smelling, "The Man With The Nose For News," shivered on top of an open milk wagon. Unlike the tall stout milkman, Sam was rather short and very slender. He had no natural padding to keep out the cold. He pulled his coat collar as high as it would go, and his hat low, over his thick brown hair. The two men chatted amiably on their way into Settle, Elly Fielding's home town. The milkman dropped Sam at the police station and continued down the cobbled Main Street.

Constable Wright was out of uniform. "So sorry, sir." Embarrassed, he jumped to attention and buttoned his jacket. "Not used to gettin' early calls at t' station, sir. What can I do fer y'?"

Sam smiled cordially. "Please, don't worry about it. I'm trying to find Anthony Roundtree."

The constable grinned and nodded proudly. "Aye, number one citizen in t' town o' Settle 'e is, sir."

"Really? What makes him so special?"

The constable yawned and stretched. " 'scuse me again, sir. Join me fer a cuppa, and I'll tell thee all tha' wishes t' know."

He put water on to boil, lumbered across the street to the bake shop, and disappeared into the rear kitchen. Sam quickly noted everything on Main Street: a butcher shop, a grocery store / post office, a chemist, a cobbler, a blacksmith / harness shop, a bakery/tea shop, and a pub. The kettle whistled and Constable Wright returned with hot buttered scones and jam.

As the food appeared, so did a large Alsatian. It held one ear up, the other down, and had an ugly scar across its head. Its brownish coat was matted and full of burrs. The dog tottered over to the constable, panting bad breath.

The constable scowled, pointing to the open door. "Get out o' 'ere, Rex!"

The dog stared at the scones and Sam laughed. Recognizing an ally, Rex hurried to Sam, gazed with adoring eyes, licked his hand, and leaned against him. Sam chuckled and crossed his arms. "SIT! Rex."

The dog sat, still staring at the scones.

7

Surprised, Sam said, "Rex, DOWN!" The dog lay down.

"Rex, CRAWL!"

The dog crawled forward about two feet and looked back with a bored face. "Rex, HEEL!" The dog hurried to sit at Sam's left. He patted Rex's head, "Good dog!" Rex banged his tail against the floor, panted happily, and stared at the scones. "Constable, did you train this dog?"

The constable shook his head. "I never saw t' dog before last week. Wandered in starvin' e' did. We all been feedin' 'im. Don't know who 'e b'longs t'. Didn' know 'e did tricks. Everyone started callin' 'im Rex. Don't know 'is real name."

"Smart dog to learn a new name that fast." Sam leaned over to examine the dog's scarred head. "Looks like he was shot, a long time ago." He scratched Rex behind the ear. "I used to train dogs." He examined Rex's bony frame. "Sure don't like to see one looking like this. He looks like a police dog." Rex raised his long nose, slurping a wet tongue over Sam's face.

When the men started on their scones, Rex won a large portion of Sam's.

The men made small talk, and Sam had to force the conversation back to Anthony Roundtree. Constable Wright's version of Elly's betrothal sounded like a fairy tale. Two great families, the Roundtrees and the Garinghams, were to be blissfully joined through holy matrimony.

Sam scratched Rex's head. "That's great. I heard that the girl ran away."

The constable laughed. "Aye, she were always a funny sort a' girl, raight wild tha' knows. She ran off for a bit of adventure, that's all, but she's cumin' 'ome today. There're 'avin' a quiet wedding, then the 'appy couple's catchin' the train fer Hull, and a boat fer Europe, fer an 'oneymoon. Tomorrow, Roundtree's throwin' a raight big party for t' whole district. Been waitin' a long time fer this. Lucky if you're still in these parts. It'll be better than t' county fair." The constable was so excited he did not notice the blood drain from Sam's face.

Sam tried to sound nonchalant. "So, how do they know she'll be home, today?"

"Oh, aye, well y' see, Miss Roundtree - that's Miss Lillian Roundtree, Mr. Roundtree's sister, she was in t' millinery t' other day, buying white satin ribbon fer a weddin' bouquet. Said 'er brother would be fetchin' Miss Elisa from Skipton, and the weddin' would be today."

Sam nervously pushed his hair from his dark blue eyes. There was a telephone on the wall. "I have some friends to contact. I wonder if I may

8

use your telephone." He reached into his pocket and dropped heavy coins on the constable's desk.

The constable sat to attention, scooping up the coins. "Well, sir, 'tis the duty and privilege of t' Settle constabulary to assist travelers. Please, 'elp yourself."

"Where is the Roundtree estate?"

Constable Wright proudly put on his helmet. "Straigh' up t' road, 'bout a mile." Politely moving out of earshot, he stood in his open doorway, inspecting Main Street.

By 11:30 a bright sun warmed the air. Sam was a bundle of nerves. He had telephoned Father Tim and Dr. Vickers. Neither had received a call from London. He tried telephoning Isabelle, and the operator told him the lines to London were all busy. He told her he was a doctor and this was a matter of life and death. The operator said she would do her best. If he will please hang up, she will try to rush the call through. He sat by the telephone, drumming his fingers and petting Rex.

He found Elly's green hair ribbon in his jacket pocket and twirled it around his finger. Rex nosed the ribbon and Sam's eyes lit up. "I'll bet you remember everything you were ever taught." Glancing out the open door, he could see the constable chatting with another man. He held the ribbon to Rex's nose, whispering, "Find Elly, old boy. Find Elly." The phone rang and he grabbed it. "Isabelle?"

It was only the operator, apologizing that the lines to London were still busy. Sam thanked her and told her not to bother trying again. He petted the dog. "It's just you and me, Rex. We've got to save Elly. You're a member of the force, boy." Rex barked and licked Sam's face.

The dog had no collar, so Sam asked the constable for a length of rope. Delighted to be rid of the smelly beast, the constable went into his back room, returning with several ropes. Sam fashioned a collar and leash, bid the constable, "good bye," and "thanks." Delighted with his new master, Rex barked happily and wagged his entire back end. Together, man and dog left the police station, trotting toward the Roundtree estate.

A strong wind pushed them along the pleasant country road. Threatening clouds gathered overhead. They passed a row of workers' cottages, came to a gatehouse, and a long, tree-lined drive. In the distance stood the big house. As Constable Wright predicted, the grounds looked like a county fair. Colourful pavilions covered the lawn and workers moved between wagons, tents, and entrances to the house. Sam smiled to himself. With this many people about, he could mingle and do some serious snooping. Rex started sniffing and barking. Was he picking up Elly's scent? Was she here already? "REX! HEEL!" He patted Rex's head and shortened the rope lead. "Good dog."

Sam remembered Elly's diagram of the house and grounds. Her room was at the back, facing into the woods. He led Rex behind the house, away from the workers. True to her drawing, a trellis clung along the back, all the way up to her second-story windows. Twisted around the thin fencing were thick, thorny canes of climbing roses. Sam looked up into her dark room. A doll slumped on the windowsill. He shook his head, imagining Elly in its place.

Rex found a stream behind the house and happily sloshed in the icy water. Sam took a drink and washed his face. He tied Rex to a tree, opened his case, took out locksmith's tools and fishing line. He checked his penknife and put everything in his pockets. He left his case, coat, and hat, and crept to the entrance of a long neglected root cellar.

Elly's directions were perfect. He was quickly at one of two back staircases, on his way up to her bedroom. Voices echoed through long passageways, but none were near enough to worry him.

Her bedroom door was locked, but he used his tools and quickly lifted the latch. He locked himself in and looked around. The space was large and bare. The floorboards were unpolished and the window curtains faded. There were a few old toys, a doll's house, a lame rocking-horse, a school desk, and shelves of books. A narrow cot was covered with old quilts. No wonder Elly hated this room.

In the center, a bed sheet covered a tall pointy object. He pulled off the sheet and jumped back. A dressmaker's dummy wore a wedding gown, Elly's size. Beside it was a small table with a wedding veil, shoes, and gloves. His palms were moist as he nervously replaced the sheet, and hurried to the two large windows.

Elly had told him she used to run away by climbing down the trellis. Desperate to keep her prisoner, her father had nailed the windows shut. That was years ago, but Sam feared she might need that escape route again. He used his pocketknife to pry a dozen nails from each window frame. The old wood was rotten, the glass was loose, and the windows rattled in the wind. He scooped the loose nails into his pocket, opened one of the windows, and leaned out. He wound fishing line around the rotting wood trellis and chunky rose canes. If Elly did climb down, it should be strong enough to hold her.

By the time he got back to Rex, it was mid-afternoon. The sun had gone and a light rain started falling. He shivered, buttoned his coat, and pulled on his hat. He untied Rex and walked toward the pavilions. A feeding station for the workers had been set up under one of the tents. Servants carried vats of food from the kitchen. A small group of dogs devoured food from a trough. Sam let Rex go and he happily joined the other dogs, sniffing and slurping.

A young woman in a maid's uniform swished her skirt at Sam. "Tha's not from around 'ere."

Laughing, he slipped his arm around her all-too-willing waist. "You're a pretty girl. What's your name?" He led her toward the food. In her company, he was less likely to be noticed as an outsider, and he was hungry.

"Mary," she giggled, a blush spreading over her pale cheeks. "What's yours?"

"Sam, and that's Rex." He pointed to the dog, head down in the trough.

She wrinkled her nose. "'es not much t' look at."

"Maybe not, but it's what's up here that counts." Sam pointed to his head.

"Are thee one of t' entertainers then? Does yer dog do tricks?"

"Your guess, Mary. So what do you do in the big house?"

"Serving maid. We're feedin' five 'undred tomorrow."

"Five-hundred? That's great! I'll go home a rich man."

She rubbed up against him. "Will tha take me wi' thee? I'm dyin' t' get away."

"Why? Don't you like your job?"

Suddenly serious, she pulled away. "T' job's all right, it's just..." She shrugged.

"Can you cook?"

"Aye, I'm learnin'."

"Well, I'm hungry." He queued with the workers and was handed a plate of hot, comforting stew. The dogs quickly devoured their supper, and chased each other around the field.

Mary batted her eyes at Sam. "I got t' go back, or cook'll be cross."

"Mustn't let cook get cross, but maybe I can see you later. What time do you get off?"

She wound a curl of fair hair around her finger, and pouted. "We'll not get off tonight. We all 'ave t' be in early, on a count a t' wedding."

Sam's stomach cramped. Forcing a smile, he leaned in close, his blue eyes looking deep into Mary's. "Well, if you can't come to me, I'm going to have to go to you."

She blushed and giggled.

Gulping down his stew, he left his plate and spoon in a large tub of dirty dishes. "Where do I go?"

Making sure she was not watched, Mary led Sam around the side of the house to a small window. She pushed it open. "'Ere's t' pantry. 'Up those stairs i' my room. They'll be wantin' us all inside when t' young mistress arrives. Cum back after nine and give a knock on t' window. If I can, I'll cum out t' thee."

Sam's jaw tensed, but he kept smiling. "The young mistress has been away?"

"Aye, she should be 'ere soon. T' master went t' fetch 'er. She's gettin' married tonight, but they don't want t' make a big show of it. A private family weddin'. No one else's invited. We won't get t' see it." She pouted, then shook her head. "When I get married, I want everyone t' see me."

"MARY! Where is that girl? MARY!"

Mary jumped. "Blu'dy 'ell! There's cook. See tha later, Sam." She jumped through the open window, closing it after her. In the distance he heard, "I been 'ere all the time, Cook…"

Sam leaned against the building, breathing hard. "A private family wedding." Of course - no one will see the bride married against her will. Maybe Isabelle got his message and Elly was safe. Maybe all his worry was for nothing. Maybe, at this very moment, Elly was having tea at Hamilton Place. Maybe… Everything he had seen and heard screamed that she was not safe. But, why a wedding gown for a secret wedding? Mary wanted everyone to see her wedding. Who would care except the bride?

Father Tim's words flooded back. "If Lillian ever hoped to get herself married, her brother saw to it that she had no dowry to offer a husband." A frustrated maiden aunt, who'd never had a wedding of her own, might care.

As quietly as he could, Sam opened the window and climbed into the hall. He silently closed the window behind him, then stood still and listened. Directly in front of him was the corridor leading to the kitchen. He could hear the cook scolding, as pots and pans banged a raucous symphony. Smells of fresh baked bread and roast meat were intoxicating.

The stairs he had climbed to the nursery were down the hall on his left, so he curiously crept along the corridor to his right.

According to Elly's diagram, he should run into a narrow staircase leading to the back of Lillian's apartment. He followed the hallway, walking on the balls of his feet to keep the floorboards from creaking. At the end of the hall, a narrow door opened onto a rickety staircase. He stepped on the sides of the crooked steps, but the old wood still groaned.

At the top of the stairs was a pleasant drawing room. The floor was covered with a worn oriental rug, and colourful paintings lined the walls. A friendly fire hissed in the grate. Elly's family portrait hung above. He studied the faces. In the center were Elly's grandparents. Both were slim with fair hair. The oldest children could have been Elly, and actor Michael Burns. Sam knew they were actually brother and sister, Charles and Lillian Roundtree. The younger boy, Anthony, had dark hair. A baby sat in his mother's lap and a toddler stood by her side. Sam wondered if the same illness had killed all three. He pictured Charles's body floating in the Suez Canal, and shuddered.

To the right was a feminine bedroom and adjoining dressing room. At first glance everything looked lovely and lacy white. Up close, he saw that the bedspread was mismatched frilly threadwork, hanging onto the floor. He touched the canopy over the bed and old lace came off in his hand. Light footsteps sounded on the stairs, and he dove under the high mattress. Seconds later, he heard a woman hum, and saw the bottom of a dark pink skirt swish past. He looked through the lacy bedspread.

Lillian was tall, pale, bony, with streaks of grey in her copper hair: a ghostly version of Elly. She carried a bundle of grey roses and sat at her dressing table. Sam had never seen grey roses and wondered if they were special to this part of the country. She chose a few, took a white satin ribbon, and tied it around the stems. Holding the bouquet in one arm, she left the drawing room and went down the rickety back stairs.

Sam crawled from under the bed and examined the extra roses. The grey petals were
dry. A chill ran down his spine as he sped from the room, downstairs and outside.

Sunlight was fading. It would soon be dark. Workers packed their belongings. A few went into the big house, but most walked down the road, past the gatehouse. Sam was ready to cry. What could he do alone, against the whole town? Suddenly, Rex was beside him. One ear up and one down, he panted happily.

Sam hugged the dog. "I'm not alone, am I boy?" Rex licked his face. The sky opened and rain fell. Sam raced for cover. He led Rex through the empty pavilions, and chose one with a clear view of the house. He slumped against a beer barrel, wound Rex's rope around his hand, and tried to relax. Rex lay across his legs. The dog's soothing warmth lulled Sam to sleep.

Chapter Three

London, a week earlier

Peg McCarthy had spent most of Christmas Eve day freezing and starving. She hid in a doorway across the street from Mrs. Porter's boardinghouse and watched the actors leave for their holiday. Lester and Todd went first, followed by Peter and Miss Lynn. Last was Meg, tarted up even more than usual, obviously meeting a special client. Snatches of cheery conversations assured her they would all be gone overnight. Rory and Elly were nowhere to be seen. Mrs. Potter and the old women boarders, Mrs. and Miss Roche, were alone in the house.

Dusk came early and Peg was dying to get out of the cold. She tiptoed inside the house through the deserted drawing room, and into the kitchen. The only visible food was a dry bread crust. She sucked it greedily, and raced upstairs to her old third floor room.

Expecting the bedclothes to be filthy rags, she was startled to see a heavy quilt covering clean bed sheets. Shivering, she kicked off her broken shoes, dove under the covers, and pulled the bedclothes around her. As her shivering slowed, her anger rose. These nice bedclothes were for Elly Fielding. Meg and Peg had never been given anything clean and warm. Elly had ruined Peg's life. Somehow, she must repay the favor. Sniggering, she remembered Elly bleeding on the theatre stairs. At least the skinny cow had shared that bit of shame and misfortune. Peg banished visions of her own baby, ripped from her body a year ago. It would be starting to walk now: her baby with theatre manager Eric Bates.

The stove had gone out, but a few pieces of coal sat in the bucket. Peg hurried out of bed on bare feet. The floorboards felt icy cold, so she slipped on her shoes, and quickly filled the stove. She lit a match and waited for the coals to catch fire. Soon, comforting warmth radiated. She stood warming her hands, when the bedroom door opened.

Mrs. Potter stood glaring."Wha' the 'ell you doin' 'ere? The coppers should be after y' for tha' torch business, t'other nigh'."

Peg glared. "That were noffin', y' old cow!"

"Noffin' y' say? Y' nearly burned down the 'ouse down. An wha' y' think y' doin' now, burnin' m' good coal? Close that bloody stove." She pushed

Peg out of the way, stumbled against the open stove, and knocked a burning coal onto the floor. The floorboards were still soaked with flame accelerant from Peg's torch and instantly burst into flame. Suddenly, the room was an inferno. Both women screamed. Peg raced through the flames, down the stairs, and out the building. She never looked back.

Running at full speed, the deserted streets seemed the loneliest place on earth. Her worn leather heels clipped loudly, without company, down hard pavement. Stopping only when her breath gave out, she collapsed, gasping against a lamp post. She gulped biting cold air. Her lungs stung as her breath poured out like white mist. Sweat drenched her frock, clammy under her thin coat, making her shiver more.

Two young roughs, half-dead from drink and cold, approached with outstretched hands.

" 'ello, pri'y. Got someffin' fer a poor bloke?" She ran away from them, straight into a third man who grabbed her, roughly pinning her arms behind her back. She fought to get away, kicking and screaming as one man rifled her pockets, stealing the small bits of change she carried. The third man pulled up her skirt, but she kicked him in the groin, sending him howling onto his back.

The second man raised his hand to slap her. She lifted her chin and bared her teeth. As his hand smashed her cheek, she bit into his fingers, drawing blood. He screamed and lunged away. The man holding her was startled enough to relax his grasp, and she raced blindly into a strange alley. She made several turns before she hid in a doorway, listening for her attackers.

Once she was sure they were not following, she took a minute to read the street signs and get her bearings. After wandering a few blocks, she turned a corner, making a beeline to the only place she knew she could find a warm corner to lay her head. It was a half-hour's walk before she saw the dimly lit pub sign: a sleeping pink cat curled around a smiling blue mouse, with the words THE PINK KITTEN painted above.

Knowing she must look a sight, she stopped, straightened her shoulders, put on a swagger and flounced through the door. After pushing aside double-heavy wind-breaking drapes, the sickeningly sweet smell of opium made her gag. Through a thick haze, she saw three men sprawled in a corner, passing a pipe, making air bubbles through a gracefully curving vat of water. The barman looked through a crowd of men and waved a greeting. She waved back, tossed her coat onto a very full rack, and looked into the nearest of many large mirrors. Pleased that the slap had not bruised her cheek, she wiped blood from her lip, unbuttoned the top of her frock, pulled it down and pushed up the top of her bosoms. Her comb had been stolen with her money, so she loosened her thick black hair, and let it fall wildly over her shoulders.

"Marguerite, my lovely. What a nice surprise." Tommy Quinn stood behind her, reflected in the glass. His eyes were glazed and he nearly lost his balance, leaning down to kiss her naked shoulder.

In perfect upper class English, she asked, "Got anyone for me, tonight, Tommy?" Her voice sounded more desperate than she would have liked.

"All my rooms are busy, just now. Christmas you know. Always brings a good crowd." He yawned, showing the ugly gap of his missing tooth.

Exhausted and frozen to the bone, she longed to warm herself by the fire. "Can I just sit a spell, then? Someone may come in."

"Usually I'd say 'no problem', but tonight..." He gestured to the men in the corner. "Those Jessies really don't like women."

Desperate to stay, she forced a laugh, and reached her fingers between his legs. "What about a bit of a suck then, eh, Tommy love?"

He giggled, wriggling against her hand.

A thin seventeen-year-old in a schoolboy tie and ridiculously short pants, shouted from the stairs. "Is that my nanny?"

Tommy turned around, shouting, "Ronald Baston, you're in for a proper thrashing if you can't behave. Go back to the school room and practice your sums."

Ronald pouted like a spoiled child and stomped upstairs.

Tommy shrugged. "I sent for one of the ladies from the other house, but they might not be able to spare one."

Peg was frantic. "I'll do it. Just tell me what he wants."

"He wants to be thrashed. I know you don't like that sort of thing."

Her stomach lurched, but she pictured Rory, then the roughs in the street, and clenched her jaw. "Tonight, I think I'd enjoy that very much." Her heart pounded and her hands clenched into fists at her sides. "Little Ronald will get the thrashing of his life."

Tommy laughed. "Good! He'll pay very well for that. Help yourself to the costume room. There's an assortment of whips..."

"I know where they are." Eyes glaring with pent up anger, she marched up the stairs.

A cosy fire warmed the elaborately decorated costume room. Hooks on one wall were filled with a variety of whips, punishment canes, leather and metal restraints. Cloaks and hoods in a variety of colours and sizes hung on theatrical costume racks. Exhausted and pleasantly warm, Peg slumped into one of several soft settees and fell asleep.

A scream woke her. It was still dark. She hurried into the hall and was nearly trampled by a parade of half-dressed men shrieking, and running outside, into the night. Last out was Tommy Quinn. He grabbed her hand, pulling her downstairs and outside, after him. They ran for several minutes before Tommy stopped for breath. He hugged Peg for comfort and warmth, sobbing.

"That boy, Ronald Baston, he's dead." He gasped, "I don't know how... what happened... I've already been in prison. If I'm caught again... it will be the gallows."

Chapter Four

London, that same day

Christmas dinner at Lord Richfield's house had been a glory of Yuletide cheer. The walls were barely visible through heavy garlands, red satin bows, wreaths, and tinsel. Elly had seen four decorated Christmas trees in the house and wondered how many there were altogether.

The lavish Christmas Eve ball had ended at daybreak. Guests went home, the family went to bed, and an army of servants cleared up, polished, and cooked, preparing for an intimate Christmas day dinner for forty. Elly had slept late and come downstairs to find the drawing room filled with opulently dressed, good humored people. Most were toasting each other with silver-handled, cut glass tumblers of eggnog and mulled wine. A few guests had been at the party last night, but most of the faces were new.

Her eye immediately found Rory, looking elegantly slim in a stylish blue-gray suit. He was standing gracefully near the sideboard, talking with two ladies who appeared to be mother and daughter. The silly daughter was coyly playing with her fan, and Elly felt a schoolgirl urge to push it up the girl's nose. When Rory saw Elly, he excused himself, took her arm and led her out of sight of the other guests. She went willingly, but stared at the floor. He tilted his head to look into her eyes. "Happy Christmas?"

She broke into a smile and looked up shyly. "Happy Christmas. Your suit is beautiful."

He looked at her new, blue taffeta frock. "You look stunning."

Both spoke at once. "I'm sorry…" "You don't…"

He said, "You first."

She took a deep breath. "You don't hate me, do you?"

"Oh, my God," his arms flew around her waist, and hers arms around his neck, squeezing each other tight. Very gently, he let her go and kissed her forehead. She stood back. He did nothing more and she smiled with relief. He said, "The eggnog's outstanding, come and have some." She smiled, as he led her back to the drawing room.

Two fabulously laid tables stood side by side in the dining room, one for adults, the other for children. Soon a dozen little bodies, dressed in their holiday best, swarmed into the room. By far the tallest child, Lucy came in walking beautifully and looking as if she had eaten a lemon. She stayed as far behind the other children as she could manage without being herded by a pack of nannies.

Elly hurried to her. "Lucy! You look beautiful, Happy Christmas!"

Lucy grimaced. "Happy Christmas, Elly. Do you like your frocks? I chose the colours."

"They're the most beautiful frocks I've ever seen. Thank you so much." Now, Lucy beamed. Elly gave her a hug and whispered, "What a 'lucky' you are to be at the fun table. I'm going to be bored to death at the other."

The tinkle of a bell made the girls break apart. Lucy sighed and went to sit at the children's table. Elly's name card was on Sir William's left, across from a Duchess, and next to a young cleric. It took her a minute to find Rory. He was further down. Isabelle had an old cleric on her left, and a distinguished looking gentleman on her right.

After the blessing had been given and the starters finished, three Christmas geese were brought in and everyone applauded. The meal was a culinary delight, but Elly's prophecy came true. She was bored to tears. No one talked of anything but horses and who was betrothed to whom. She remembered last night's Christmas eve ball, and the witty conversations of Jeremy O'Connell and Sam Smelling.

After Christmas crackers, paper hats, and flaming Christmas pud', everyone went into the drawing room. Children and adults were quickly engaged in games of Blind Man's Bluff and Squeak Piggy, Squeak. When they tired of games, and some of the smaller children had fallen asleep, the company gathered around the piano for carols.

In a husky baritone, Sir William announced that he and Lucy would present, *Good King Wenceslas*. Lucy flushed with excitement as she stood in the crook of the Steinway. Sir William made a grand gesture of sitting at the piano and clearing his throat. His large hands descended on the poor unsuspecting keys in a combination of tones they had never experienced. He sang loudly, under pitch, and Isabelle sprang onto the bench beside him. "Bill, darling, 'Don't hide your light under a bushel,' go stand where everyone can see you. Allow me to accompany." He chortled, kissed her on the cheek, and went to stand with Lucy. Isabelle took a deep breath, looked at the music and played.

King Wenceslas and the Page sang their parts. Isabelle's right hand was heavy helping her husband to stay on pitch. She relaxed when Lucy took over. The girl's soprano was as pure as a choir boy.

Several people took turns at the piano, sometimes two or three at once. Most songs were lustily roared by the entire group, but a few were solos. Best was Elly's, *O! For The Wings of A Dove*. She had been shy to sing until Rory said, "Come on scaredy-cat, I'll play." Taking easy command of the keys, he played expressively. After a few tentative measures, she sang with the same joy she remembered, singing at school.

The last musical offering was from Isabelle and her three redheaded daughters. Lucy and Isabelle sat on the piano bench. Little Cindy and Bella stood in front. Lucy and Isabelle played a duet of the Welsh lullaby, *All Through the Night*. The second time through, they sang in close harmony, and the little ones joined in the refrain.

Sleep my child, and peace attend thee,
ALL THROUGH THE NIGHT.
Guardian angel, God will send thee,
ALL THROUGH THE NIGHT.
Soft the drowsy hours are creeping,
Hill and vale in slumber sleeping,
God alone his watch is keeping,
ALL THROUGH THE NIGHT.

The song ended and the room was perfectly still. Sir William had tears in his eyes. He hugged his wife and daughters, then turned to his guests. "Was ever a man given such a Christmas present?" The room broke into applause, fond embraces, and wishes of, "Happy Christmas!" Sir William took Isabelle into his arms and kissed her tenderly.

Elly hugged herself and looked at the floor.

Rory asked, "What's the matter?"

"I want to be loved like that."

He sighed, "You are."

She gratefully kissed his cheek.

Sheets of rain poured from the grey sky, and a canopy of umbrellas sheltered the guests as they ran from the house to their cars and carriages. When the last horse had pulled away, the servants hurried down the backstairs, wet and shivering. Only Smythe the butler stood like a sentry, waiting until the last carriage was safely around the corner, out of sight.

Almost reaching shelter, Smythe was annoyed to see a large black car pull up, splashing through a deep puddle in front of the house. The car door opened and two men in business clothes hurried up the front stairs. Smythe raced back, intercepting them before they could ring the bell. After they had spoken for a moment, he led them inside.

Chapter Five

The festivities were finally over. Delighting in peace and quiet, Sir William Richfield relaxed on a long sofa in front of his drawing room fire. Isabelle lay across his lap, with her head under his chin. Her long legs stretched across the sofa, her shoes askew on the floor.

Elly and Lucy giggled together by the hearth. "Mummy, I'm taking Elly to see the new rabbit."

"All right, dear. Mind it doesn't bite you, like the last one."

"This one won't bite." She took Elly's hand, and led her from the room.

Sir William looked after the girls. "It seems we have another daughter."

"Do you mind?"

"Not a bit, as long as we keep trying for a son."

She smiled fondly, as he leaned over and kissed her.

The butler hurried in. Seeing his master and mistress in an intimate pose on the sofa, he stopped and turned toward the wall. Sir William sighed. "What is it, Smythe?"

"Forgive me, M' Lord, M' Lady, but two gentlemen from Scotland Yard have just arrived."

Sir William blustered. "Good Lord! Don't they know it's Christmas? What do they want?"

"Something to do with a young man, sir. They asked to see Your Lord and Ladyship."

"What young man? Oh, for God's sake. Tell them to come back tomorrow."

Sitting up, Isabelle noticed the butler's soaking jacket and trousers. "Smythe, please ask the gentlemen to come in. After that, you'd best find yourself some dry clothes."

"Very good, madam. And thank you." He hurried away, shivering.

As Isabelle crammed her feet back into her shoes, Sir William stood up. "How dare they? This is frightful, absolutely frightful. Can't a man enjoy a moment's…"

A tall, grey-haired man with a large moustache strolled purposefully into the room. Even holding a soaking bowler hat and wearing a shapeless raincoat, the man had a commanding presence. A younger, shorter man, similarly dressed, followed close behind. The elder man held out a warrant card.

"Sorry to disturb you, M' Lord, M' Lady. Dreadful weather, especially for Christmas. I'd rather be home, myself, by a warm fire, but unpleasant business doesn't wait. I'm Chief Inspector Hayes, from Scotland Yard. This is Sergeant Taylor."

"What do you want?" Refusing to look at him, Sir William huffed, plopping into an armchair.

Used to being snubbed by the upper classes, the Chief Inspector took his time. After folding his warrant card into his vest pocket, he comfortably placed his hands behind his back, rocking on thick soles of large, sturdy boots. The young sergeant tucked his soaking bowler hat under his arm. He reached clumsily into his coat pocket and found a rumpled notepad and a pencil stub. Nervously licking the dull carbon tip, he opened the notepad, dropped his hat on the floor, bent over, dropped the notepad, retrieved both the hat and notepad, and slid the hat back under his arm, all the while trying not to stare at the beauteous lady-of-the-house.

Appearing bored, Isabelle gracefully spread her satin skirt, folded her hands in her lap, and gazed blankly at the floor. When Sir William finally looked up, the Chief Inspector stopped his rocking. Reaching carefully into his coat pocket, he drew out a piece of heavy note paper. "Do you recognize this, M' Lord?" He handed it to Sir William.

"Of course I recognize it. It's an invitation to our Christmas Eve ball. We sent out two-hundred of these." He angrily passed it to Isabelle.

She read the name on the card. "Ronald Batson. He's the nephew of Lydia, The Duchess of Monmouth."

The young Sergeant gasped. "Bli' me! You were right, sir, 'e was a gentleman, like…"

The Chief Inspector cut him off. "Are you well acquainted with the young gentleman, Lady Richfield?"

"No, we never met. His aunt is a friend of mine. She told me that her seventeen-year-old nephew was visiting from India, and asked that he be allowed to escort her here, Christmas Eve. Next week he's to be interviewed for Oxford. Since my invitations had already been sent, I wrote this one myself, purely as a courtesy. Last evening, the Duchess arrived alone. She pretended not to be cross, but I could tell that she was. She said her nephew had found new friends and was off 'sowing wild oats'."

Sir William forced a laugh. "Clever lad! At seventeen, a good pint and a good wench are highly preferable to the company of one's stuffy old Aunt."

Isabelle stiffened slightly.

The Sergeant made scratchy sounds, writing with his pencil.

The Chief Inspector took back the invitation. "Thank you, M' Lady. Your butler told me there are young people visiting the house. Perhaps they are acquainted with the young man."

Isabelle chuckled softly. "I think not. The Duchess's nephew and our young guests travel in very different circles."

"Nevertheless, I would like to speak with them."

Sir William stood up, blustering, "Well, you may not speak with them. I..." He started toward the men, but stumbled to a halt as his wife silently stood and pulled the bell cord. Huffing angrily, he turned away and pretended to look out a window. They were all silent for the moment it took a footman to answer. After asking him to fetch Rory and Elly, Isabelle stared icily at her husband, and sat back down. Accustomed to waiting, the Chief Inspector calmly returned to his rocking posture. The young sergeant tried to assume the same pose, but realized he would drop everything, all over again.

The footman found Rory hiding in the library. Sure he would be banished from the house as soon as the festivities were over, he had buried himself in a book. Obeying the footman's summons, he soberly walked downstairs to the drawing room. Startled to see official looking, plainly clothed men, he wondered if he was being arrested for shagging Sir William's wife. He nodded soberly. "You sent for me, sir?"

"Yes, m' boy. These gentlemen from Scotland Yard think they have some business with you."

Rory thought he would pass out.

Sir William turned to Chief Inspector Hayes. "Miss Fielding is with my little daughters, in the nursery. Surely we can we get this over, without her."

The Chief Inspector smiled politely. "It's best to wait until both are present, My Lord. It saves repeating information and possibly missing something important, a second time 'round."

Annoyed, Sir William plopped back into his armchair. A moment later, Elly and Lucy appeared together. Sir William waved his daughter away. "Lucy dear, be a good girl and go back upstairs."

"Please, Papa, I want to…?"

Isabelle softly commanded, "Do it, Lucy."

The girl clenched her jaw, turned about-face, and marched away.

Isabelle patted the sofa cushion next to her. "Elly."

Fighting the urge to bolt, Elly looked at the two threatening men. Had her father sent them? Had they come to take her home? Was Isabelle going to lie, and say Elly was her cousin? Hoping for protection, she sat very close to Isabelle.

The Chief Inspector looked from Rory to Elly. "I apologize for any inconvenience, but I need to know if either of you are acquainted with a young man named Ronald Baston?"

They glanced at each other, then shook their heads.

Sir William forced a smile. "Well, then - that's that!" He stood to usher the men out the door.

"Not quite, sir." The Chief Inspector waved the paper invitation. "The young man met with foul play last evening." The room fell still. He smiled condescendingly at Isabelle. "The details are very unpleasant, M' Lady, so it might be best if you and the young lady…"

Isabelle glared. "I'm sure the details will be equally unpleasant for the gentlemen. Please continue."

Startled by her bold words, the sergeant dropped his pencil, then picked it up again.

"As you wish, M' Lady." The Chief Inspector's face remained placid. Only a glimmer of admiration shone behind his eyes. "The young man's body was discovered, stuffed in a bag of wool, outside a brothel." He allowed a moment of silence, before continuing. "Most of his clothing was missing. This invitation was in the pocket of his coat, which had been wrapped around the body. Other than this, we have no idea of the young man's identity. Since none of you ever laid eyes on Ronald Baston, I shall have to approach the Duchess's household, in the hopes of a positive identification."

Isabelle closed her eyes. "Poor Lydia."

Sir William fumed. "Well, whoever he was, he was a damned fool. There are enough respectable houses in…" Isabelle turned her head, making him pause, then bluster more. "At seventeen, a lad needs a bit of…"

The Chief Inspector cut him off. "This particular brothel was frequented solely by men."

The room fell silent again.

26

"We have a search underway for the brothel owner..." The Chief Inspector checked the name from a paper in his pocket. "...one Thomas Quinn, and a female accomplice, Marguerite Lamoor."

The blood drained from Rory's face. "Oh, dear God."

Elly turned to him. "That's Peg."

The Chief Inspector looked at Rory then Elly. Deciding the young man looked more frightened than the young woman, he questioned Rory first. "Are you acquainted with Thomas Quinn, sir?"

Rory shrugged. "I know who he is. Tommy Quinn used to be an actor. I've seen him, but we've never spoken. I'm an actor." He gestured to Elly. "We're both apprentices at His Majesty's Theatre. I had heard that Mr. Quinn was running a pub."

"He was, in a way. At least the lower level seemed an ordinary sort of pub. The upper rooms were quite extra - ordinary."

Rory shook his head. "But, what was Peg doing with Tommy Quinn?"

"Do Marguerite's friends call her Peg?"

Rory shook his head with disgust. "Her name is Peg McCarthy. She made up the name Marguerite Lamoor. No one calls her that." He paused, struck with a new idea. "At least no one I know of. If she's involved with Tommy Quinn she may have a secret life I know nothing about."

"You seem to be well acquainted with the young lady."

Rory coloured. "I am."

"Chief Inspector!" The sergeant excitedly flipped back pages in his note pad.

"I'm ahead of you, Taylor."

Disappointed, the sergeant's smile faded. Shuffling his feet, he turned back to his current page.

The Chief Inspector turned to Elly. "Miss..." He read her name from his note,

"...Fielding. Are you acquainted with Thomas Quinn?"

"No, sir. I've never heard of him. But, I've only been in London a few days. I know Peg, though." She took a deep breath. "Monday night, she lit a torch in my face."

Everyone stared at her.

"I wasn't hurt -- just frightened. Some of my hair was singed. It needed to be cut off."

The Chief Inspector was sceptical. "Why wasn't this reported?"

Rory looked puzzled. "I'm sure it was, sir. Eric Bates, the theatre manager, he said he'd take care of…" A cold chill went up his spine. Bates couldn't turn Peg in. She knew too much. She could ruin him.

"'He'd take care of' what, Mr. Cook?"

Breathing heavily, Rory stared at the floor. "With all due respect, Chief Inspector, Mr. Bates is my employer. It is not my place to make assumptions about his actions. It would be best if you approached him on the matter."

He nodded. "As you wish. It happens that we are currently seeking the whereabouts of a Peg McCarthy, who burned down a boardinghouse, last evening."

Elly stared up. "What boardinghouse?"

"Not, Charles II Street?" Rory's eyes were like saucers.

"Number 5 Charles II Street, to be exact. Are you familiar with it?"

Elly's voice was almost a cry. "We live there, with the other apprentices. Was anyone hurt?"

Looking at Elly's expensive frock and beautifully dressed hair, the Chief Inspector shook his head. "I think you are mistaken, Miss. You must be confusing it with another boardinghouse."

Rory gave a half laugh. "Don't let these borrowed clothes deceive you, Chief Inspector. We live there. Now please, was anyone hurt?"

Surprised, he checked his notes again. "The Proprietress, Mrs. Samantha Potter. She jumped from a window and died hitting the pavement."

Elly gasped. "That's horrible. Was anyone else hurt?"

"Two old women escaped out the back. There was no one else in the house, at the time."

"Oh, thank God." Her hand flew over her lips.

Rory moved next to her, leaning on the sofa's arm rest. "That's right. Everyone was going to be away for Christmas."

"Can you give me the names of the other residents?"

"Gladly." Beads of perspiration formed on Rory's brow. "They're actors, mostly. Two young chaps, Lester Reid and Todd Sinclair. Lester's father's a vicar, somewhere near Penzance. Both lads were going there for Christmas. An old man, Peter Stirling, and his lady friend, Mrs. Lynn, were going to her daughter. Another girl, Meg O'Malley, was off with some bloke. The old women are mother and daughter, Mrs. and Miss Roche. How bad was the fire? Is the place still livable? Not that it was ever livable."

"With the fire and water damage, it's been condemned. The first two floors are still standing. The old women refuse to leave."

Elly whispered, "What will happen to them?"

"If they don't move of their own accord, they'll be forcibly removed. They must have some income, to be paying for their keep. If they can't pay for lodgings, they'll be taken to a poorhouse."

Elly let out an involuntary gasp.

Rory's heart pounded. His face had turned chalk white.

The Chief Inspector folded his notes. "Should I need to question you two further, where will you be residing?"

Rory shrugged. "I've no idea. Eric Bates will have to find us new digs. You can always find us at the theatre. We start rehearsing a new play this week, so we'll be there twenty-hours-a-day."

"Very well." He looked over his shoulder. "Taylor!"

"Yes, sir?"

"See to the car."

"Yes, sir." The sergeant tried to cram his mangled notebook into his coat pocket, then dropped his pencil. As he bent to fetch the pencil, his bowler hat slipped from under his arm, falling to the floor. After securing his notepad, pencil and hat, he nodded to everyone and hurried out, leaving a trail of water.

Almost imperceptibly, the Chief Inspector shook his head. He looked back into the room. No one had moved. "Again, I apologize for disturbing your Christmas."

Isabelle smiled sadly. "I'm sure this is not the way your family envisioned their Christmas, either."

He sighed. "Actually, Lady Richfield, they've become used to it, over the years." He watched Sir William walk to the liquor cart. "Good night, sir. Thank you for your cooperation."

"Good night." Without looking up, Sir William poured himself a brandy.

The Chief drew a card from his pocket and handed it to Isabelle. "If you ever need my assistance, madam. For anything at all."

She took the card, smiled slightly, then raised an eyebrow. "Thank you, Chief Inspector. I hope we never shall."

"Good night, M' Lady." Pausing longer than necessary, he smiled back, turned and walked out of the magnificent mansion, into the storm.

Chapter Six

Sir William handed Rory a balloon of brandy. "Here, m' boy."

"Thank you, sir." Rory downed it in one gulp and Sir William was surprised.

"Another?"

"Umm... No, sir. Thanks."

Sir William offered one to his wife. "Izzy?"

"No, thank you, Bill." She looked at the rain puddles left by the policemen and rang for the servants. "Rory, is there anything you need to do?"

Some colour came back into his cheeks. "I don't know. I...I really can't believe this." He stood up and set the glass on an end table. "I need to go and see it, for myself."

"Is there anything you two left at the house? Anything you need?"

Elly twisted her mouth. "I had a school frock, hidden in the attic. But there isn't any attic, now." She touched her blue skirt. "This frock is ever so much nicer. You've been very kind."

She looked so sweet and vulnerable, Sir William felt compelled to protect her. He smiled back. "Not to worry, my dear. Frocks are easy enough to come by." He turned to Rory. "And you, my boy?"

Rory's body was stiff, his breathing shallow. "No, sir. At least, there's nothing of monetary value, but there is something." He looked very embarrassed. "No, it's... It's nothing."

Sir William downed his brandy. "Come along, we can take my car." He started toward the door.

"There's no need for you to bother, sir, really."

"It's no bother. I want to see this place, or what's left of it." He turned back. "Izzy, we won't be long."

She nodded. Elly started to stand, and Isabelle pulled her back down. "You're going nowhere, my girl."

Elly called, "Rory! What will happen to Peg?"

He stopped in the doorway. "She'll hang -- if they catch her." His face tensed, as he

hurried from the room.

*

30

The windshield wipers were of little use, as Sir William's chauffeur strained to see through heavy rain, pelting against the glass. When the car finally pulled in front of number 5 Charles II Street, Rory hesitated, taking a moment to stare at the place he had called home for a-year-and-a-half. Even through the heavy downpour, he could see that the top floors were crumbled cinders. The bottom floors looked like the same dilapidated ruin they had always been. Glancing at the sidewalk, he was grateful the rain had washed away any evidence of a broken body.

He braced himself, hurried out of the car, and scrambled up the broken steps, only to be met by a police CONDEMNED sign, nailed to the door. Below it was another notice instructing residents to vacate the premises or be forcibly evicted. Under that, a rain smeared note told employees of His Majesty's Theatre to report to the bursar's office for relocation information. Rory pushed the door open. Sir William followed him inside, took a cursory look around and wrinkled his nose. "How long did you live here?"

Rory laughed disparagingly. "Far too long, sir."

"You were slated to move out, anyway. You're going on salary, aren't you?"

"Mr. O'Connell said that I was. I haven't heard word one from Eric Bates, and his wife holds the purse strings. This disaster doesn't bode well for me. Mr. Bates will never find another boardinghouse as cheap. He'll have to pay more to keep us, and may decide he hasn't the extra, to pay me wages."

"That would be very unfair."

"Yes, sir. I hope I'm wrong."

Rory walked through the dark narrow entranceway and followed the light from two single candles, into the dismal drawing room. Miss and Mrs. Roches sat wrapped in coats and scarves, next to an ice cold stove. The ancient Mrs. Roche shivered, staring vapidly into space. The elderly Miss Roche hugged herself, rocking back and forth. When she saw Rory, she keened softly and continued to rock. His previous loathing for the woman melted into pity. Suddenly remembering Sir William, he turned back.

"Please come in, sir – if you can stand it. The chimney pipe seems to be intact. I'll just try to light the stove." He found an old newspaper and crumpled several sheets, stuffed them into the stove, then covered the paper with coals from a nearby bucket. He lit the paper, waited until the coals caught fire, then secured the iron door. Warmth started to cheer the

31

smoke blackened room, but the old women seemed unaware there was a change.

Not knowing what to say to them, he forced a smile. "Well, good bye then, Miss Roche, Mrs. Roche. Good luck." He guessed they would both be dead within the week. Eager to leave, he turned back to Sir William. "Thank you, sir. There's nothing here. You were kind to bring me. We can go." His voice caught and he coughed to cover his embarrassment.

Sir William watched the old women. "Isabelle's a champion of social causes. I'm sure she knows someone who can help those two. Would they take assistance, or are they too proud?"

Rory remembered Miss Roche insulting him again and again. "In the past I would have said..." He shook his head. "I don't know." He started out the door.

"Wasn't there something you wanted?"

"It's nothing of value, but... yes, there is something."

He moved to the foot of the stairs, lit a candle stub, and carefully examined the broken steps. Picking his way gingerly, stair by stair, minding the broken boards, he climbed to his second-story room. The walls were charred and wet, both from rain and the fire brigade's hoses. The bed was partially collapsed. He crouched down, careful not to soil his trousers, and cautiously reached underneath. His hand searched through a pile of wet rubble before pulling out a soaking, battered leather schoolbag. He walked back to the top of the stairs and stopped, planning his descent. Coming down was trickier than going up. His feet slipped on the wet boards and a charred step broke under his weight.

Sir William stood at the foot of the stairs, hands extended, ready to catch Rory if he slipped and fell. Once Rory was safely down, Sir William looked curiously at the schoolbag. "That's it, then?"

"Yes, sir." Almost overcome with emotion, he swallowed. "This is my only worldly possession. Before Christmas, I had one decent, borrowed suit." He smiled ironically. "Now, thanks to you, I have three. One is on my back and the others are at your house. You've been very kind to Elly and me. We owe you a great deal."

Sir William put his hand on Rory's shoulder. "Not at all, my boy." This slight kindness was almost more than Rory could bear. Seeing that the young man was about to cry, Sir William briskly removed his hand. "Let's be off then. Shall we?"

"Yes, sir." Rory ran out the door, clutching his schoolbag. The two men were silent on the short drive back to Hamilton Place.

Warm and safe, inside the mansion, a servant took their wet coats. Frantic with worry, Elly raced out to meet them. "Rory! Was anyone there? What was it like? Do Lester and Todd know about...?"

Sir William caught her arm, leading her upstairs. "My dear girl, that place is a nightmare." He gestured for Isabelle to look after Rory.

Still clutching his schoolbag, Rory gritted his teeth to stay composed. He waited until Elly and Sir William were upstairs and out of hearing, then carefully set down the bag. Too emotionally charged to speak above a whisper, he clenched his fists.

"Thank goodness Sir William can answer Elly's questions. I couldn't bear that just now." He stared at the floor. "Oh, Isabelle, it was horrible. Everything was black and ruined. Those old women..." He shook his head. "They were cruel and nasty and mean and I hated them, but I never wished them harm. Now, Mrs. Potter's dead. The others are worse than dead. If they go to a poorhouse, they'll starve."

Isabelle's face was full of concern. She longed to comfort him, but knowing he could not accept tenderness without breaking down, she stayed where she was.

Frantic to keep control, he turned away from her caring eyes. "I fancied Peg, once. Then I hated her. Now she'll hang. Everything that I... everyone I touch... something bad happens to them."

Isabelle moved towards him. "That's nonsense. You..."

He held up a hand. "You'd better stay clear of me. I'm bad luck for everyone."

"Stop – talking – nonsense! Stop it at once."

His body throbbed, as he tried controlling his emotions. "It's my fault Peg attacked Elly. Mrs. Potter might still be alive if I'd..."

"Do you suddenly have a crystal ball that foretells the future?"

"Of course not, But if..."

She clutched his shoulders. "Rory, listen to me."

Squeezing his eyes shut, he forced back tears.

"Are you listening?"

He nodded.

"You – have – done – nothing – wrong."

He shook his head.

"Nothing!"

"But... if I'd stayed at Oxford, none of this would have happened. I broke my mother's heart when I left. We were very close."

"None of this is your fault. Isn't it just possible that you've done some good along the way? What would have happened to Elly if you hadn't been here for her?"

He shook his head, then grabbed Isabelle. She held him tight, forcing back her own tears, stroking his wet hair, and sighing with relief when his heart began to slow. His breathing became more regular. Muscle by muscle, he relaxed in her arms. Finally, emotionally drained, he stood back, breathing deeply.

"I'm a shambles. I'm so sorry." He took a handkerchief from his back pocket, wiped his eyes and blew his nose. He put the handkerchief away and looked into her startling blue eyes. "My God, what a Christmas." They laughed, uneasily. He looked up the stairs. "You don't mind if we stay another night? I thought you'd want us gone... Me gone, at least."

"Bill had his doubts about you. He's come around."

"Elly's all right?"

"She's fine. Bill's a good father."

Rory sighed. "I imagine you'll be spending tonight with him."

"Oh yes." She smiled. "He's more than earned it."

"He's very kind."

"He's wonderful. And, your young lady will be waiting for you."

Very lightly, he ran the side of his hand down her cheek.

She stepped away, smiling warily. "Another time, sweet boy."

He carefully picked up his soaking, battered schoolbag and glanced at the elegance of his surroundings. Unable to deal with the incongruity, he shook his head, hurried across the parquet floor and bounded up the stairs, two at a time.

Isabelle watched him go, smiled to herself, walked gracefully across the foyer and upstairs to her husband's room.

Chapter Seven

December 26, 1903

The next day, Rory Cook sat on the edge of a dark, red-leather chair in Sir William Richfield's study. A shaft of bright sunlight reflected off a huge polished-mahogany desk. Book shelves lined one wall, while dark-walnut panelling covered another.

Rory leaned over a triangular corner table, holding a telephone-earpiece in one hand and its candlestick shaped body in the other. "Mr. Collins, good morning, sir, this is Rory Cook. I... Yes sir, it was trag... Yes, sir." Still listening, he put his hand over the mouthpiece and glanced at Elly Fielding, standing eagerly beside him.

He grabbed a pencil off the desk and leaned over a notepad, writing information dictated by the bursar at His Majesty's Theatre. "Yes, Mr. Collins, Darry House... 12 Morris Street, between Haymarket and Market Streets..." He smiled up at Elly. "Yes, sir, I know the street. It's a continuation of Panton, going south west, on the other side of Haymarket. It's very near the theatre..."

He wrote some more. "Jack and Mabel Hogan... Sorry, sir? Once again, please?" He looked worried. "I'm not registered there? But, Mr. Collins, I *am* an apprentice. We were all living at Mrs. Potter's..." He was quiet, listening for a moment. Suddenly a smile flashed across his face. "Yes, sir! With two-pounds-a-week, I can most certainly pay for my own lodging. Yes, sir. Thank you, sir. I'll be by later. Good bye, then."

Rory put the earpiece back into the curved-wire-holder mounted on the side of the telephone. He sat still, grinning at Elly. Knowing what he was going to say, she waited, smiling in anticipation. He chuckled to himself, then held out his hands. "I'm an actor. A real actor, on a real salary. Finally!" They threw their arms around each other, laughing and hopping in a clumsy dance. "We'll just tell Lord and Lady Richfield. Then we'll go."

*

The bursar handed Rory eight crowns. "You're on your own now, Mr. Cook. Two pounds a week won't be keepin' y' well off. There's a decent boardin' house by Millar's Pub, or y' might try Darry House, where the apprentices are goin'."

"Thanks, Mr. O'Rourke." Rory studied the silver coins in his hand. "Two pounds in my pocket and I feel like a rich man."

O'Rourke looked over his spectacles. "Yer fer real, now, laddie. Yer an actor. Well dun. Congratulations!"

"Thank you, sir!" Rory shook the old man's hand, turned and threw his arms around Elly. "My God, I'm an actor, a real actor!"

She beamed. "You always were. Everyone knew it but you."

He looked into her shining eyes. "Come on, let's take a look at your new home." The two young people skipped out, into the cold sunshine.

Darry House was four streets from the theatre, on the way to Jeremy's flat. It had a bright red brick face, clean windows with white lace curtains, a scrubbed stoop, and a legible sign out front.

DARRY HOUSE
Mr. and Mrs. Hogan, Proprietors

Elly squeezed Rory's hand. "This looks too good to be true."

He rang the bell and laughed. "Even the bell works."

The door opened, and a portly, middle-aged gentleman smiled brightly. His suit was clean but slightly frayed. "More actors? Come in, come in!"

Rory stepped back, letting Elly walk ahead. The man clipped a pair of pince-nez on the bridge of his nose and read from a paper on a desk near the door. "Hmm, are you Margaret O'Malley or Elly Fielding?" Rory and Elly burst out laughing. The man looked over his glasses. "Didn't know I was a comedian."

Rory said, "I'm sorry, sir. You'll understand the joke once you meet Meg, um, Miss O'Malley."

"Righty-o," he looked at Elly. "So you must be Elly Fielding."

"Yes, sir." Suddenly shy, she coloured slightly and curtsied. She glanced up and caught the man's eye. A silly smile came over his face and his eyes seemed to glaze over. Rory noted Hogan's reaction, bit his cheek and studied the wallpaper. It was a cheerful blue and white.

"You must be Peter Sterling." They burst out laughing again, and the man shrugged his shoulders. "I only have the names of three gentlemen, and the other two are already here. Is Sterling coming? I got word this morning that he wasn't."

Rory said, "I couldn't say, sir. We haven't seen Peter since before the holiday."

"Who are you, then?"

"Rory Cook, sir. I'm an actor."

"Well, do you want his room, then? I'm damned put out," he looked at Elly. "Pardon my language, Miss, but I turned a shop assistant away this morning, thinking all my rooms were let. I'm Jack Hogan, but I assume you gathered that."

"Yes, sir -- but wait a moment. You said, 'his room', sir. Is each one to have his own room?"

Hogan put two fingers on the bridge of his nose, removing his pince-nez. "Of course, what do you think I'm running here, a brothel?"

Rory sputtered a laugh. "No, Mr. Hogan, certainly not."

Hogan raised one bushy eyebrow, a restrained smile on his generous lips.

"...but you see, sir, I'm a poor actor, and have to pay from my measly salary..."

"How much are they paying you, then?"

Rory hesitated.

"I'm in the mood to be generous, boy-o, take advantage of it."

"Two pounds a week, sir."

"All right, I'll give you room and two meals a day for a pound a week, and my wife's a good cook." He waved a finger. "No one goes hungry at Jack Hogan's house!"

Rory whispered to Elly. "That'll be different."

Hogan continued. "Y' bring down your bed linen first Saturday of the month, pick up the clean that afternoon, and make the beds yourselves. All right?"

Elly's eyes were wide, begging Rory to accept.

"That'll be fine, sir. Thank you."

"All right, Rory - Cook..." he wrote down the name. "...and Elly Fielding. Welcome home." Hogan extended his large warm hand and both accepted it gratefully. "Mabel's at the shops, you'll meet her later." He picked up two keys from behind the desk and handed one to Elly. Changing his mind, he took it back and gave it to Rory. "This room's on the second floor, next to Mabel's and mine. I was young once. I don't want you doing what I did... in my house." He winked at Rory, who coloured slightly. "Young lady, you'll be on the third floor." Hogan gave Elly the other key. "Come along, I'll show you 'round."

The house was simply decorated and spotlessly clean. A long hall led straight into a large dining room. To the right was a cozy drawing room and to the left, the kitchen. A fire crackled in every room, sending delicious warmth in all directions. Upstairs, the bedrooms were tiny, but neat and clean.

Rory was hungry but Elly was too excited to think about food. Last evening she had received the most extraordinary letter of her life. After Sir William and Rory returned from Potter's, a messenger had arrived with a letter and a script for *THE MAGISTRATE*. Smyth had found her with Lord Richfield. Elly had looked dumbly at the envelope until his prodding made her open it. She read aloud,

Dear Miss Fielding,

I trust you have had a pleasant holiday. I enjoyed our conversation last evening and our dance.

You may have heard that Peg is no longer associated with His Majesty's Theatre. Her role in MACBETH has been covered from within the company. You will now cover, Beatie, in THE MAGISTRATE. While you may never go on, you should be prepared to do so as soon as possible. I am going to coach you myself.

I know you have seen the play. Please read it, all of it, not just your part. Do nothing else before we meet, NOTHING. Do not attempt to act it out, or even read it aloud.

We will work tomorrow at 3:00 in the rehearsal hall.

My regards to Lord and Lady Richfield, and my thanks to them for a delightful Christmas eve.

J. O'Connell

Elly's mouth fell open, and Sir William smiled. "That's good news I believe."

She smiled back. "Yes, sir, it is."

"Capitol, go to it."

Elly carefully placed the letter between the pages of her script. She clutched it to her heart and ran up to her room. She read the play twice through, falling asleep with it in her lap.

It was afternoon by the time Rory and Elly moved their clothes into Darry House. A clock softly chimed one o'clock: an agonizing two hours until her coaching at 3:00. She looked around her new room. It was so small the door opened within inches of a narrow bed with a cherry red spread. A gaslight hung on the wall above her pillow. A wardrobe stood across from the bed, a small desk and chair sat by the window, and a mirror hung on the wall. She looked out the cherry red window curtain onto the tree lined street below. A candlestick sat on the desk, a pitcher and basin underneath. There was no stove, but the room was warm, thanks to a warm brick wall that she guessed housed one of the chimneys.

She stood in front of the wardrobe and opened the double doors. They pulled out about four inches and were up against her face. It was impossible to pass between the bed and the open doors. She closed the doors, stepped to one side, and opened one door at a time. Now, she could hang her frocks on one side, then fold her gloves and linen into drawers on the other side.

There was a knock on the door. She called, "Come in!" and Lester's friendly face appeared.

He looked at her room. "This is exactly like mine."

"Really? Let me see." She followed him to the room next door. It was a perfect copy.

He chuckled. "Must have been a special on red linen."

"Isn't this place wonderful." They sat on his bed. "If only it hadn't happened the way it did."

Lester shook his head. "That woman was horrible, but no one deserves to die like that. Peg's in big trouble this time."

"I hope they don't find her."

"Why? I think you, more than anyone, would want her safely put away."

Elly bit her lip. "She was kind to me once. Where's Todd's room, and Meg's?"

"They're both upstairs. Is Rory staying here? I know he's on salary, lucky bugger." He flinched. "Sorry, bad word."

Elly smiled sadly. "You've been here longer than he has. You should have been put on salary first."

Lester shrugged it off, but she could tell he was hurt.

"Rory's room is downstairs."

"Good, I'm glad he's here." Lester's smile was genuine.

"Mr. Hogan didn't want him upstairs."

"Why?"

She coloured slightly. "He told Rory, 'I was young once, and I don't want you doing what I did, in my house'."

Lester's eyes went wide, then closed as he started to laugh. "Oh, God, did he really say that?" He continued chuckling, then abruptly stopped and shook his head. "Hogan trusts me. What a bore." He looked adoringly at Elly. "Character men are always the last. Last to get salaried, last to get loved."

"Ooh!" She leaned over and gave him a hug.

*

The clock struck 2:30 as Elly and Rory arrived at the rehearsal hall. "It's awfully early." Rory looked around. "Are you sure you want to sit here for half-an-hour?"

She wrung her hands. "I just didn't want to be late." She paced stiffly. "I'm so nervous." She looked around the large bare room. The walls were pristine whitewash, but the bare wood floor needed sweeping. A wonderfully musty odour filled her nose, as sunlight poured through the windows, illuminating bits of flying dust. Chairs were pushed against one wall, two tables against another, and an old piano stood in a corner. She smiled, remembering acting class when the room was full of people.

Rory did not look happy. Her throat tightened. "Are you angry with me?"

He let out a big sigh and looked up. "Of course not. But I am jealous. I've been here a year, and O'Connell's never given me a private coaching."

Her hands clutched together. "I'm sure he's only helping me because it's an emergency, and I'm so dreadful."

"You're not dreadful. Quite the opposite. But it is 'an emergency'. Eddy always puts in the understudies, but Eddy's no teacher."

"I'm sure that's the reason."

She was so sweet; he couldn't help but smile back. "Do you want me to read with…"

She stepped back, alarmed.

"No! Right!" He stood to attention. "You're not to speak a word, I remember. I do understudy 'Cis', and will probably rehearse with you, but…" He held up a warning finger, "…not today."

She tried to smile, but her lip trembled.

"Don't fret so. You'll be fine."

"'Never contradict and never agree.' That's what they say about him, right?"

He chuckled. "That's right, or at least it used to be. He seems mellower these days. Could be an illusion. You'll know soon enough."

Her eyes went wide.

40

"Stop worrying. He likes you."

She swallowed. "He's been kind to me, but he still frightens me."

"He likes people to be frightened of him. That's how he controls them, keeps them out of his private life." He shook his head, remembering the night he stayed at Jeremy's flat. "You can't control him, so you may as well relax."

*

"THEN WE'LL BLOODY WELL HAVE TO PAY FOR IT!" Hilda Bates could be the most pigheaded woman on the planet. Pennywise and pound foolish, after a decade of working together, she still mistrusted Jeremy O'Connell's judgment. It was he who brought in audiences and made her a small fortune. He had saved her husband's theatre, all those years ago, yet she still fought him. "I WANT THAT MOUNTAIN!" His voice sounded marvellous, bellowing through the hall as he left her office and bounded up the stairs to the rehearsal hall. His sharp footsteps clipped loudly as he entered the opened doorway. His boots were highly polished and his new pinstriped suit hung beautifully on his long frame. Rory Cook and Elly Fielding sprang to attention.

Jerry pointed to Elly. "How is the new boarding house?"

"Lovely, sir."

"Mr. Cook?"

"First class, sir. Of course, we haven't had a meal yet."

"Let me know tonight. I want to hear personally from everyone staying there."

"Yes, sir. I'll pass the word, Sir!"

"Thank you, Mr. Cook."

Jeremy thought Rory was going to salute. Instead, he nodded and started to leave. "Mr. Cook!" He made an about-face. "It is almost 3:00. Come back at 4:30 and read 'Cis' with Miss Fielding."

"Yes, sir." He winked at Elly and left the room, closing the door behind him.

Jerry turned to Elly. "So, Miss Fielding, have you read the play?"

"Twice, sir. Not a word out loud." Her voice was a whisper.

"Good." He smiled and pulled two chairs into the center of the floor.

She watched him with glowing green eyes, stood absolutely still, and clutched her script. He turned towards her and her gaze lowered. She was terrified.

He shook his head. "Come along, Elly. I'm not going to bite you."

41

"No, sir." Her cheeks flushed as she took the chair he offered.

He chuckled, "Not just now, at any rate." Her face grew redder and he laughed full out. "Oh dear, I shouldn't tease you so." He sat down, casually opening his perfectly pressed suit jacket. "You embarrass so easily, it brings out the schoolboy in me."

She looked up to see his eyes dancing and a finger over his smiling lips.

Releasing a nervous laugh, she looked him straight in the eye. Even in an old school frock, with her fabulous hair hidden behind her back, she was stunningly beautiful. Taller than most women and slender as a willow, light red hair framing perfectly symmetrical bone structure, she reminded him of a Renaissance angel. He picked up the script. "Page three, if you please." She opened her script. "We are going to look at each other and say the words. Just say the words. All right?"

"Yes, sir." Ankles and knees tight together, she held her script high enough to watch him over the top.

He kept his voice and face expressionless. *"Beatie!"*

Taking a breath she put on her brightest smiled. *"Cis dear, dinner isn't over, surely?"*

Jerry closed his eyes. "Just say the words, Elly -- nothing more."

Her smile vanished. She swallowed and tried the line again. *"Cis dear, dinner isn't over, surely?"* Her reading was still affected and false, so he stopped again. Her body stiffened.

"Elly." He pushed down her script. "Look at me and say the words."

She spoke with no thought of what she was saying. *"Cis dear, dinner isn't over, surely?"*

Jerry nodded and continued reading. *"Not quite. I had one of my convenient headaches and cleared out…"*

Her next three lines were repeated in the same torturous manner. By the end of the scene he was no longer stopping her, but she was reading with no expression whatever.

"So, my dear, what did that feel like?"

She looked horrified. "Honestly sir? I feel like an idiot."

"That's fine, let us go again."

By the end of the second read through, she felt much calmer and the words were finding a natural rhythm.

Jerry smiled. "Better. How did that feel?"

"It was interesting." She gave a nervous laugh.

"How so?"

"Well, sir," she paused, finding the right words. "When we started, all the words came from here." She pointed to her lips, then rolled her eyes. "Of course, where else could they come from?"

He chuckled and watched her thoughtfully. "And now?"

She took a big breath. "By the end, the words were coming from here." She touched her abdomen. Her eyes went wide and she broke into a smile. "Right now, talking to you, the words are coming from here."

"Good. Now, tell me everything you know about Beatie."

She swallowed. "I don't know much about her." Her eyes narrowed as she concentrated. "We're told that she's *'A young lady reduced to teaching music,'* and that she came to the Magistrate's attention through a crime of some sort."

"What sort, do you suppose?" Jerry relaxed into his chair and took out his cigarette case.

Wonderful ideas poured out of the girl. "Well, if she used to be well off, perhaps her father was an embezzler and lost all his money, and was brought to court, and the Magistrate who's very soft hearted, saw Beatie in the stalls, discovered that she's musical... Oh, and her father was sent up... and her mother's dead... so now Beatie teaches music to Cis and other children the Magistrate recommends her to?" She waited for approval.

Jerry lit his cigarette, raised his head and inhaled deeply. "I like that."

She sat back, relieved.

He exhaled and smiled. "Very clever. So, in this scene with Cis, what does Beatie want?"

"That's easy. She wants to be taken care of. She wants to be loved and protected."

"You say that with certainty."

"Yes, sir."

"You are familiar with those wants?"

"Yes, sir."

"And yet you ran away..."

"I was never loved and protected, sir." All the day's tension exploded into tears. "Quite the opposite. Forgive me." Weeping, she started to stand. He took her arm and held her in the chair.

"Use those tears, Elly. Forget for a moment that this is a comedy. Beatie has those feelings, too." They started the scene again, and she sobbed her way through the first lines. By the scene's close, the tears had dried. She seemed confused, but Jerry quickly moved to Beatie's other scene and they

43

read it through. After that, he told her to take a break and spend ten minutes in the sunshine. She obeyed, returning after eight minutes.

When they reread the scenes, she felt confident enough to ask, "Did that sound like a comedy?"

"It sounded real. That's plenty for you to think about right now. You have a naturally silly streak, which will make you very good at comedy, eventually. Don't try to be funny, that will come of its own accord."

Slightly before 4:30 Rory appeared. He sat down and read the scenes with Elly. When they were done, he looked at Jerry. "I can't believe it. Congratulations, sir." He smiled at Elly. "You were all right, really all right."

She bit her lip and smiled back.

Jerry asked, "What's today, Saturday? -- The Scottish play tonight, *MAGISTRATE* tomorrow matinee. Monday's a day off. Do you two mind working on your day off?"

They were both eager to continue.

"Let me see the two of you here, Monday at 3:00." He started to leave. "Rory!" He looked up and Jerry offered his hand. "I almost forgot, welcome to the company."

Rory beamed and firmly shook his hand. "Thank you, sir."

"Since I'm at leisure until rehearsals for *THE TEMPEST* begin, is there anything you'd like to work on?"

Rory's mouth dropped open then turned up in a smile. "Oh, yes sir, a dozen things."

Jerry laughed. "I'm not sure I have time for a dozen."

Rory coloured. "Sorry sir, didn't mean to sound hoggish, but I desperately need help with Hamlet."

"Hamlet?" Jerry nodded in approval. "Ambitious, good for you, it'll be a pleasure." He thought for a moment. "Of course for Hamlet, I should give you over to Simon Camden. He had far more success with the role than I ever did."

Rory's face lit up then dropped. "Is he as good a teacher as you are?"

"Very politic."

"I'm serious."

"I know you are, dear boy, and I honestly don't know the answer. He's an outstanding director, so I imagine he's also a good teacher, but the two don't automatically go together." Jerry looked at the two young actors. "I should get him over here to do some coaching, at any event. He's taking

44

the winter to raise money for a year's tour of India, so he could make himself useful. It's good for all of you to have someone else's perspective. Elly, you met Simon Christmas Eve; came on a bit strong, didn't he?"

"Yes, sir." She shuddered at the memory, and he chuckled. "Not to worry, he's harmless." He reconsidered. "No, with you, I dare say he's not harmless." He cocked his head. "But you would have a splendid time. Feather in your cap, perhaps?" *What a marvellous idea. If I give Elly to Simon, he might leave Katherine alone.* There was a twinkle in his eye as he turned to go.

The colour had drained from Rory's face.

Elly asked, "May we work on *THE MAGISTRATE* on our own, before Monday?"

Jerry thought for a moment. "Better not. Continue reading the whole play over, and make up more background for Beatie. You did well today." He beamed Elly a radiant smile and she sent an equally radiant one back. "Mr. Cook, I'll see you on stage. Miss Fielding, I'll see you later on." He nodded his head, started out, and turned back. "I want reports on the boardinghouse."

Chapter Eight

Darry House seemed miraculous. This clean, tidy boardinghouse was a ten minute walk from the theatre. At Mrs. Potter's they had slept three-to-a-bed. Now, everyone had their own tiny room. Lester, Todd, Rory, and Elly had a happy reunion, while meeting nine other boarders. The six men and three women worked in nearby shops and offices. The other boarders were friendly, but cautious, talking to theatre people. They found it very odd that they were coming home from a long day's work, and the actors were on their way out. The boardinghouse served one breakfast at 6:30 a.m. Now, there was to be a second breakfast at 9:00 a.m., for the five actors.

Lester smiled warmly and looked around the table. He was short and chubby, with a round face and a mass of curly black hair. "Have any of you lot seen a play at His Majesty's?"

Only the landlords and two of the borders had been to the theatre, so Lester chuckled, "Well, the rest of you are in for a treat. I'm Lester Reid. My father's a vicar and this gathering reminds me of Sundays at the vicarage -- happy times." He shook hands all around. Everyone seemed to like him.

Mr. Hogan smiled. "We've got tickets for Sunday's *MAGISTRATE* matinee. It sounds like a good laugh."

"Indeed it is. You won't be disappointed." Lester touched Elly's shoulder. "This lovely is Elly Fielding, our newest acquisition, just come on for our next production, *THE TEMPEST*." Elly smiled and nodded politely. The others smiled back.

Lester moved behind Todd. "And here's my gangling friend, Todd Sinclair."

Todd giggled a low, "How-d'-you-do." He reached a remarkably long arm and shook hands with everyone.

Rory leapt up before Lester could say something embarrassing about him. "I'm Rory Cook. It's a pleasure to meet you all." He nodded politely at the nine borders. Rory was rather short, but blond and very handsome. The three women borders smiled back.

One-by-one, the borders introduced themselves. They were just finishing when Meg flounced into the room, calling loudly, " 'ow d'j do everyone.

So sorry t' be late." The four actors cringed with embarrassment. As always, Meg's frock was cut too low and her skirt too high. Her bleached yellow hair was dry as straw, and her skin was stained with makeup. She looked like a tart.

Lester was quick to intervene. "This, my new friends, is Margaret O'Malley. Quite the character, our Meg is." He put his arm around her shoulder, laughed fondly, and invited everyone to think of her as a sort of pet.

They were saved further embarrassment when platters of food arrived, and were quickly passed around the table. The actors were thrilled. Instead of dry bread and cold drippings, there was roasted meat, whole potatoes, vegetables, and soft bread with a real crust. No one left the table hungry.

*

A week later, Elly dressed in a pale-blue frock Lady Richfield had given her. She arranged her hair especially nicely, and carefully walked downstairs. Rory met her on the landing. "You look lovely. What's the occasion?"

Elly smiled proudly. "Sam Smelling is taking me to lunch."

Rory sneered, "That ass of a journalist?" When Elly pushed gently past, he sighed, "I'm sure the food will be good. I wish I had his money and connections." When she didn't respond, he teased, "Maybe I should find a rich woman and be her fancy man." When she still didn't respond, he rushed past her, down the stairs and out the door, in the direction of Hamilton Place.

Minutes later, Sam helped Elly into the hansom, climbed in behind her, and closed the door. As the cab lurched forward, he smiled. "I hope you're hungry."

"I'm so nervous, I'm not sure I can eat."

"If you can't, I'll take someone else." He called up to the driver, "Stop the cab!" The horse pulled to a halt.

She stared, laughing with disbelief. "You're terrible."

"I know." His blue eyes were dancing under his tousled brown hair. He called up, again, "Drive on, Cabbie!" Sitting back down, he pushed his hair from his eyes. It immediately fell back. "Still nervous?"

"Much less."

"Getting hungry?"

"Yes." She smiled back. "Thanks, Sam."

"For what?"

"For making me laugh."

"You need to laugh."

She lowered her eyes.

"Like, right now." He lunged to tickle her and drove his fingers into whalebone. "Oww!" He shook his hands. "You still wear those instruments of torture? No wonder you can't eat."

"I'm sorry, did it hurt you?"

He rubbed his fingers.

"Don't they wear them in America?"

"Older women do. The younger ones, less-and-less."

"Wouldn't that be wonderful. I can't even imagine that kind of comfort -- to go all day without a corset."

"Try it some time."

"Really? You wouldn't mind?" She twisted her mouth. "How stupid of me. Obviously, *you* wouldn't mind. Other people might."

"What other people?" Still in pain, he flexed his fingers.

She looked down shyly. "Oh, I don't know."

"Seriously, who's opinions do you value enough to suffer for?"

"Everyone." She looked up apologetically. "Anyone at all. I'm a wretched coward."

"I don't think that's true at all." He spoke seriously. "You've been trained to comply, like all upper-crust British ladies, but you've got more nerve than most."

"Do I really?"

"Yes."

"I'm so pleased you think so."

"Most ladies don't dance in green velvet one minute, then fall asleep in charwomen's rags the next."

She put her hand over her mouth. "I was so embarrassed. I was sure Mr. Bates was going to sack me."

"How can he sack you, if he's not paying you?"

"He can put me out on the street. The new boardinghouse is expensive. I hear he's not happy about it."

Looking very sad, he shook his head. "Poor Cinder-Elly."

Her eyes flashed as she playfully slapped him on the arm. He lurched back in exaggerated fear and laughed as the carriage pulled up to Simpsons.

Elly felt like royalty when one white-gloved doorman held the carriage door, and another opened the wide door to the restaurant. The small, elegant lobby had a parquet floor. The walls were lined with gild-framed mirrors and fantastic flower arrangements. Pristine linen cloths, glittering silverware, cut glass, and more fresh flowers adorned the tables. As the maitre D' held Elly's chair, she could feel the eyes of curious patrons burning holes in her back. She glanced over the menu and shuddered. Some of the items were in French, and she hoped the prices were in francs, rather than pounds.

Sam fluttered his hand, looked down his nose, and asked the waiter where a certain fish had been caught. He sounded exactly like Jeremy O'Connell. When the maitre D' stammered that he did not know, Sam slowly closed the menu and said that the chef could choose their meal. Looking relieved, the maitre D' bowed and walked away.

Elly put the napkin over her mouth to keep from laughing. "That was the most brilliantly funny thing I've ever seen. Why aren't you on the stage?"

Delighted by her reaction, he laughed and relaxed back into Sam. "I'm a good mimic, that's all. I could never think of anything original, and I'd be bored after the second performance. I have a good eye. It makes me a good investigator." He sat back. "Did you see the *DAILY MAIL*, by the way?"

"No, why? Do you have an article in it?"

He nodded.

"What's it about?

"It's called, 'A London Christmas Eve'."

"...about Lady Richfield's party?"

He nodded.

"Is it funny?"

"I think so, and sweet. You'll like what I wrote about you."

"You wrote about me?" Her eyes were like saucers.

"Who did I spend most of the evening with?"

She raised her eyes to heaven. "Oh, dear, and I acted like such a ninny."

"You were a regular person in a mansion full of phonies. You were delightful."

Throughout the meal, Sam plied her with questions about personalities and relationships at His Majesty's. Unused to being treated as an adult, she was flattered by his serious attention. She surprised herself with the multitude of images she had in her mind. Dodging questions about her former life, an hour-and-a-half of delightful tastes flew by.

Back in a hansom, bouncing toward *THE MAGISTRATE* matinee, her full stomach was in pain from her corset stays. She was eager to ask Katherine about giving corsets up altogether.

When they neared the theatre, Elly became serious. "Sam, you're famous, aren't you?"

He looked surprised. "Does it matter?"

"Well, no. It's just that, well, I don't want to say something stupid, if someone asks me about you, and I know they will."

He raised an eyebrow. "Among journalists, I'm well respected. Is that a good enough answer?"

She nodded.

"What else?"

Embarrassed, and sorry she had brought the subject up, she shrugged her shoulders.

He thought for a moment. "I'm not married."

She blushed.

"...although I've been unofficially engaged for fifteen years."

She stared at him.

"I'm twenty-eight, by the way."

She swallowed.

"I proposed to my boss's daughter when I was thirteen and she was twelve. I had a job after school, setting type at her father's newspaper." He put on a pained expression. "Rebecca." Looking up, he put his hands together. "Dear God, please find Rebecca a husband, so she'll forget about me." He pretended to cry. "I've been praying for that for fourteen years. It hasn't happened, yet. I love Rebecca, like a sister, and she's been a great sister." He looked back at Elly. Her mouth was shut tight and her eyes were like saucers. "What else?"

She shrugged her shoulders.

"My father's a police detective, and my mother was an actress, before she married my father." He lowered his brows. "She gave up the wicked life to marry Officer Richard Smelling, New York Police Department; 6th Precinct; Canine Unit. Yes, Smelling is my real name."

She giggled.

"My father's a good man, loves dogs. Made guard dog trainers out of his three sons. My mother's a saint for putting up with a house full of boys and dogs." He looked at Elly, grimacing slightly. "How old are you?"

She mirrored his expression. "Eighteen."

He flinched.

"Last Tuesday."

He put his hands over his face. "Oh, God."

"Is that bad?"

He twisted his mouth and looked up in exaggerated concentration. "There's nothing we can do about it." He yawned, "You know, I hadn't seen Isabelle in two years. It was awfully nice of her to invite me to her party. I met her in New York, at the race track. Bill had two horses running."

Elly looked up. "They took horses all the way to America?"

"He has good horses. They did all right."

"Do you like horses?"

"I do, but I was there investigating a crime syndicate that had been fixing races. It was an ugly business. Two great horses were crippled, an owner stabbed, an ace jockey mysteriously broke his neck." He rubbed his chest. "I still have a scar from a knife wound."

"Somebody stabbed you?" He yawned again, so Elly continued, "Why?"

"Umm?"

"Why were you stabbed?"

"Oh, I learned the truth."

"Were you badly hurt?"

He laughed. "I was bleeding like a pig. At the hospital, I refused to lie down. It made everybody crazy, but the moment was too precious. I had to get the story out. It was *my* story and I wasn't going to let anyone else share the credit. I'd almost died for it and I wanted the glory. Rebecca arrived with a typewriter and convinced the doctors to let her stay in the room while they sewed me up. I dictated and she typed." He smiled at the memory.

Elly had gone pale. "Rebecca sounds wonderful."

"Oh, she is."

"Did you get the glory?"

"Oh, yeah!" He put his head back and laughed. "Every major paper in the country wanted that story. Suddenly 'The Man With The Nose For News' was being read from-sea-to-sea. Telegrams poured in and I haven't had a day's worry since. It seems I can do no wrong. I cable something to my New York agent about three-times-a-week and he always finds a buyer. Most of what I write is good -- some of it is fluff."

"Do you write every day?"

"Nearly. I'll never forget the first time I saw Isabelle." His eyes looked slightly out of focus as he stared happily into space. "She was wondrous." He sat back and pushed the hair off his face.

Elly looked into his dark-blue eyes and giggled. "You look like you're in love."

"I am." He shook his head and his hair fell back. "It was love at first sight. It wasn't just that she was beautiful. I'd never seen a woman with that kind of class. Don't get me wrong, I've known every kind of woman." He was silent for a moment, focusing the memory. "Ever been to a race track?"

She shook her head.

"Well, in America, the horses run in a great big circle, and the spectators watch from bleachers." Seeing Elly's blank expression, he thought of how to explain. "It's kind of like steep theatre stalls, only a lot bigger." Elly nodded, and he continued. "Isabelle was sitting in the owners' section, with a lot of other people. It was a windy day, and things were blowing all over the place. Peoples' hats flew off, papers scattered, but the wind didn't touch her. She was perfectly still.

"The other women were dressed in loud colours and flashy clothes. She wore the simplest, most elegant suit I'd ever seen on a woman. It was almost the same colour as her hair, only a darker reddish-brown. She wore almost no jewellery, and no makeup that I could see. But those blue eyes... People spoke to her. She smiled, answering politely. She was pleasant to everyone, but even from a distance I could see she was keeping her comments short, and constantly deferring to her husband. Bill was strutting around, bragging about his stable, and how much better everything was in England. He would have been obnoxious if he weren't so charming. He made everyone laugh.

"I was posing as a runner, the lowest-of-the-low, carrying bets to the bookies, and it was a particular bookie I was after. I looked awful. Ratty old suit, broken shoes, two day's growth of beard. No one gave me a second look, except Isabelle. I was working undercover with a police detective who was posing as an owner. I needed to pass him a message, so I snuck up to the owners' section, stashed my note in the arranged place, and was about to leave, when I happened to see her drop her guard, just for a second.

"Her eyelids closed like moons eclipsing bright blue suns. The moons lifted and she looked up, directly into my eyes. Realizing I had caught her, she smiled at me like a conspirator, then turned her head and went back to her role of dutiful wife. Later, I asked who she was, and someone said, 'English Bill's wife.'"

Elly laughed.

Sheepishly embarrassed, Sam shrugged. "We're crass Americans. What can I tell you? Over the next couple of weeks I saw her twice more, just in passing. I don't know if she saw me. Then, when I was fresh out of the hospital, a politician's wife was giving a gala birthday party for a foreign friend. My story had made me the hottest new thing in town, so I was invited. I didn't want to go, but Rebecca found out about my invitation, swore she'd never get to go to 'one of those parties,' if I didn't take her to this one. She cried, saying that I owed it to her for getting my story out, which of course I did, and she drove me nuts until I agreed.

"We got to the party, and the guest of honour was 'English Bill's wife,' La-dy Is-a-belle Rich-field." He almost sang the name. "The party was awful but Rebecca loved it, and the time I spent with Isabelle was wonderful. She recognized me at once. It was amazing." He smiled at the memory. "My God, she was charming. She turned thirty that night. Soon she'll be thirty-three."

When they reached the theatre, Sam and Elly entered through the wide front doors. Elly had never come in with the paying audience. It felt exciting. While passing the actors' photographs, she stopped in front of a new one: a sweet faced young woman with long dark hair parted down the middle. The name, SANDRA LINFORD, was written underneath. Elly remembered Eugene speaking of, "the lovely Sandra." It was her letters that Michael did not throw away.

Climbing the stairs to Eric Bates's box, Elly heard Isabelle's mellow laugh, then saw her electric blue eyes flash at Simon Camden. He leaned on the rail and laughed back to her. When he saw Elly, his smile softened and his eyes ran down her slender body. He offered his hand to help her down the step. Good manners made Elly lightly touch his fingers. Her arms prickled with goose flesh as she gazed into his laughing blue-gray eyes.

"Isabelle, this child's frightened to death of me. What shall I do to remedy it?"

"Come now, Simon, there are any number of things you can do, if you really want to. Hello Sam." She offered Sam her hand. "Thank you a hundred times. You've made me the queen of London."

"You were always the queen of London, Isabelle," He bowed, kissed her hand, and pushed the hair away from his eyes. "Thank you for giving me such a juicy party to write about." A copy of the *DAILY MAIL* lay open on a seat and Elly sat down to read it. Below the title, "A London Christmas Eve," was a cartoon of a nose and the words, "by Sam Smell, 'The Man With The Nose For News'."

True to his word, it was very funny and sweet. It was like seeing the whole party over again. He managed to poke fun at everyone without being unkind to anyone. The only person he ridiculed was himself, presenting an American bumpkin among upper crust British society. About Elly, he wrote, "...I had often heard the phrase, 'English rose', but had never actually met one until the lovely Elly Fielding suffered my goat-like attempt at the waltz. Her charm and good humour kept the goat from becoming an ass. I trust her poor toes have healed from the bruising my hoofs inflicted."

She finished the article, then glanced at the other side of the paper. Her heart skipped a beat. Among the art gallery notices:

Premier Exhibition:
ROBERT DENNISON
Oils and Pastels
Gildstein Gallery
January 5th - 10th

Isabelle watched her read the notice. "That's very nice for your friend."
Short of breath, Elly tried to smile. "Yes, it's wonderful."
Sam saw the colour drain from Elly's face. He picked up the paper. "This fellow's a friend of yours?"
"Yes. He's an awfully good painter."
"Any paintings of you?"
"Yes!" She sat up excited. "He says it's his best piece..." her smile vanished.
Isabelle said, "Elly dear, come to tea tomorrow. We'll talk then."
The house lights began to dim and everyone found chairs.
Isabelle looked toward the stairs. "I wonder what happened to Rory? He was going to check in backstage, then join us."
Just before the house went to black, the center curtain parted and Eddy Edwards stepped out, wearing a suit. He looked up nervously and cleared

his throat. In a nasal voice he called, "In this afternoon's performance, the role of 'Cis Farringdon' will be played by Rory Cook. Thank You." He nodded awkwardly and disappeared behind the curtain.

Isabelle almost screamed with excitement.

Simon put his arm around Isabelle, whispering into her ear, "What makes you so interested in this young chap?"

She whispered back, "He's the girl's friend, and I - like - him!"

He chuckled. "My dear Mrs. Richfield, you're soooo naughty." As the house went to black, he kissed the back of her neck.

Chapter Nine

January 5, 1904

Two hours before the first rehearsal for *THE TEMPEST*, Elly was kidnapped. Back at the boardinghouse, Lester had knocked on Elly's door, calling. "Breakfast time, Forrest Nymph." When there was no answer, he tried her door. It was unlocked. Inside, her bed was freshly made. He knew painter Robert Dennison was in town, and guessed Elly had spent the night with him. Rory was ferociously jealous of this man he had never met, so Lester didn't mentioned Elly's absence.

After breakfast, Rory, Lester, and Todd walked to the theatre, joining other actors in the rehearsal hall. Donald Moran called, "Come on you lot, get your scripts."

The actors took their scripts, nervously joking to relieve tension. Ross Hamlin, playing the monster Caliban, took stage. He was short and stocky, with a long nose. Shaggy hair fell around his face, making him look like a sheep dog. He was quickly surrounded by other actors, laughing hysterically as he acted out a funny story. When Sandra smiled at him, he raised his hands like paws and panted.

The trill of Katherine's laugh brought him to his feet. "Ross, you're terrible. I thought Simon was bad."

Ross put his hands over his heart. "Kathy, comparing me to Simon, even as a lecher, is praise indeed." He raced to kiss her and saw Jeremy O'Connell walk through the door. "Look out lads, schoolmaster's here."

Jeremy stopped, turned very slowly, and spoke with exaggerated dignity. "It is always rewarding when a prodigal actor returns from the intellectual rigors of the Pantomime."

Everyone laughed as the men embraced. Sandra Lindford sped toward Jeremy, throwing her arms around his neck. "Thank you for Miranda, thank you, thank you."

Jeremy hugged her back, looked down at her beautiful heart-shaped face, silky dark hair, and sparkling dark eyes. His casting was excellent. She was a talented actress and looked like she could be his daughter.

"No thanks needed, m' dear. You'll be lovely." Chuckling, he added, "Or if you must thank someone, thank Katie for refusing the role." He glanced at Katherine, softly laughing as she arranged papers on the long director's table.

Stage-manager Eddy Edwards called out, "Ladies and gentlemen, please take your seats."

Jeremy sat behind the long table. His new assistant, Katherine Stewart, sat on his left and Eddy Edwards on his right. He felt strange having Katherine next to him, and guessed it felt even stranger for her. This was the first production in a lifetime of theatre work, when Katherine's responsibilities would be entirely off-stage.

The cast of actors: twenty-two men, one boy, and two women sat in a semicircle facing the table. Nine-year-old Evan grinned like a Cheshire cat. He had finally convinced Jeremy to let him play a cabin boy.

There should have been three women. Jeremy scowled. "Where is Elly Fielding?"

Before he could fly into a rage, Katherine grabbed his arm. "She has no lines, Jerry. Whatever she needs to learn, she will learn quickly. Please, your *actors* are all here."

He sighed, then smiled in spite of himself. Katherine's diamond ring still nestled in his breast pocket. Like a burning ember, it seemed to blast heat through his chest. He longed to have the thing out in the open and imagined forcing it onto her finger in front of the entire company. He also imagined her rejecting it in front of the entire company. The ring stayed hidden.

Taking his time, Jeremy explained his concept for the production, and specific qualities he needed from each of the principal actors. "I would be a fool not to make use of the striking resemblance between Mr. Burns and Miss Fielding. While her nymph will mostly be Prospero's reflection and conscience, with the cunning aid of wardrobe, I will weave some magic making the audience see double."

Michael Burns pursed his lips. "I assume she will be the Water Nymph?"

"Precisely."

Michael glared at his script and Jeremy wondered why. The water nymph had no lines.

Jeremy finished his instructions and looked over his troop of immensely talented actors. He felt proud and fearful: proud they were working for him, and fearful he might not be able to control them. Every actor had a strong personality, wonderful imagination, and the ability to create an exciting character without his aid. He expected some actors to discover better character choices than he had imagined. The first read-through would show whose ideas mirrored his, and whose did not. Before this afternoon's second read-through, any major differences must be resolved.

He smiled with a clenched jaw. "Ladies and gentlemen, please, before we begin: just listen to each other and say the words. The cleaner we can begin, the sooner *my* concept can be created, and little or no bloodshed need occur."

There were slight smiles, but no laughter. He expected Katherine to grimace and was surprised when she calmly opened her script. "As you know, Miss Stewart has declined the role of Miranda in deference of a younger member of our ensemble." He nodded at Sandra and she smiled back. "But, I am privileged that Miss Stewart is sharing her venerable gifts as production assistant, acting coach, and calming influence for the star."

Katherine's composure broke. She laughed and everyone joined in.

The actors opened their scripts. Eddy read the stage directions as the actors read their lines. Every time an actor displeased Jeremy, he marked his script. All-in-all, the actors did well. The lines were read and the story simply told. Jeremy was satisfied with this first read-through.

The set designer showed them a model of the set, explaining his storm at sea and some magical effects. The costume designer spread her magnificent watercolour sketches along three tables. Eddy called a break, and Jeremy went to Eric Bates's office for a conference with dour financial manager, Hilda Bates.

The meeting took longer than expected. Jeremy returned to his director's table frustrated, hungry, and thirsty. He was ready to battle through the scenes he had marked in his script, and was startled to see no script. In its place were a chicken salad sandwich, sweet lemon tea, and vanilla biscuits. Katherine appeared, smiling calmly, holding his script. She sat next to him as he devoured the delicious lunch. He left a few crusts, which Evan snatched for the theatre cats.

Finally, Jeremy opened his script, found his first set of black marks, and called the actors involved. He expected to tediously rehearse the scene, over-and-over, until they got it right. When they listened to his instructions and read the scene exactly as he wished, he was astounded. He scratched a note to himself, broke a pencil point, and cursed. Much to his surprise, a delicate female hand gently removed the broken pencil and handed him a sharp one. The next scene correction was equally painless. As his tea cup emptied, the same lovely hand refilled it.

The third scene was not as easy to fix. His mouth became dry and a sliced orange appeared beside his script. The second read-through was nearly flawless and the third, wonderful. Stupidly unaware of the reason, he smiled naively and thanked everyone for their sensational work.

With one voice the actors shouted, "Thank you, Kathy," pointed to Katherine and applauded her. She sat back, happily laughing, accepting their praise.

Jeremy stared at her. "You took my script and coached them, during the break."

She calmly nodded. "I did."

"You made them understand what I wanted."

She nodded again. "I did." When Jeremy stared in admiration, she burst out laughing.

"Your actors are very intelligent, Jerry. It wasn't difficult. I explained simply and slowly, that's all." Her china-blue eyes shone with amusement.

*

Lady Richfield's maid came to her mistress's bedroom carrying a tray of tea and toast. "It's eleven o'clock, M' Lady. You've got the Suffragist luncheon at one."

Isabelle opened one very sore eye. "Oh dear, Charleston. Is it time already? I didn't get to bed until six." She rolled over and buried her head in a pillow. "Do I have to go? Those women don't need me."

The maid giggled. "Y' don't have to, M' Lady, but I know you'll feel badly later on, if y' don't go."

"You're right, Charleston." Isabelle turned over and stretched. "You're always right."

"Was the dinner a success, M' Lady?"

"It was," Isabelle sat up and held her suddenly aching head. "There's going to be a whole wing built on the free school, just for girls. It turned out better than I ever could have hoped."

"That's wonderful, M' Lady."

"The evening started terribly. A pompous ass took the podium, insisting all our resources should go to the boys' school. Then Chief-Inspector Hayes spoke and, thank God, turned everything around. He talked about being a young officer patrolling the slums, and watching little girls become prostitutes because they were starving and had no place to go. Our school will house twenty girls, give them free room and board, and a comprehensive education until they reach fourteen. After that we will try to place them in suitable positions. I hope we can expand every year."

Charleston stood proudly. "I was fourteen when I went into service for your mother, Lady Hereford. I've come all the way from chambermaid to lady's maid."

"You've done marvellously well, Charleston. I would have been lost without you, all these years."

Isabelle was not moving, so the maid pulled off her warm bedclothes. "I've a bath ready, M' Lady, if you'd like one now."

Isabelle shivered. "Good idea." She hurried into the comfort of warm sudsy water.

While her mistress luxuriated, sipping milky tea, Charleston gently sponged her back. "You know, M' Lady, I remember the Chief-Inspector. He came here Christmas night. He looked just like the Scotland Yard men in the novels: tall with gray hair and a beautiful, large moustache."

Isabelle sighed, "That was the worst night of my life. It had been an absolutely perfect Christmas day. Then Smythe raced in, saying two gentlemen from Scotland Yard were at the door. Bill was furious. A moment later, Chief-Inspector Hayes and his sergeant marched in." Isabelle held the sides of the bathtub and carefully stood up.

Charleston dried her with a soft towel. "All of us servants snuck looks, but we could just see the gentlemen come, and go again."

Isabelle chuckled. "Well, as you say, Chief-Inspector Hayes is indeed a good-looking man, and his manners are beautiful. That night, he gave me his card. I called him yesterday. Blessedly, he was able to convince that wretched school board to educate girls."

Isabelle was nearly dressed when she noticed the pile of paintings her young daughters had left her. She chuckled fondly, studying each elaborate effort. A slip of paper fell out, onto the floor. "What's that, Charleston?"

The maid handed Isabelle the note from Smythe. She read the few lines,

Your Ladyship,
Sam Smelling called from Grassington 9 - 8, at 6:00 this evening. He
wants you to know that Elly Fielding is in danger and needs protection
immediately.
Smythe

Isabelle caught her breath, raced downstairs, and telephoned His Majesty's Theatre. She asked for Katherine Stewart, saying it was urgent. While she waited, she closed her eyes trying to control her racing heart.

"Isabelle?"

"Kathy, is Elly there?"

"No, and Jerry's furious. He…"

"Where is she?"

"I don't know?"

"Does anyone know?"

"Why, what's happened?"

"Sam called from Yorkshire last night. He said that Elly's in danger and needs protection immediately. Does anyone know where she is?"

*

Katherine's heart was in her mouth as she ran back to the rehearsal hall. Interrupting the actors, she asked, "Has anyone seen Elly Fielding?"

Jeremy was annoyed. "Why, what's happened?"

Katherine blinked back frightened tears, "Who saw her last?"

Michael said, "She spent the night at our flat, but I saw her slip out early this morning. Last night she said she'd get breakfast at Darry House, and go to rehearsal from there."

"Well?" Katherine looked to the other apprentices.

Lester said, "She wasn't there this morning."

Rory looked pale. "Isn't she at the art gallery?"

Katherine raced back to the phone. "Isabelle?"

"Yes Kathy, where is she?"

"She spent the night with Dennison, but left the flat very early this morning. She was headed back to the boardinghouse, but apparently never got there."

"Could she have played truant, and spent the day with Dennison?"

"She'd never have done that."

*

Isabelle took a deep breath. "Try not to worry, Kathy. I have phone numbers for Sam. He should be in Settle by now. If she's on her way there, he'll be waiting for her. My solicitor called late yesterday. He's had a telegram from Egypt, affirming that Charles Roundtree was probably murdered, but definitely alive when Anthony Roundtree married Elly's mother. Papers are being drawn up, turning Elly's guardianship over to Bill and me. I'll notify a friend at Scotland Yard and we'll be on a train to

61

Settle within a couple of hours. I'll call as soon as I have any news. Go back to work, darling. That's what she'd want. Bye, now."

Isabelle hung up, counted to ten, and jiggled the phone handle. She telephoned Gildstein Gallery and spoke to Robert Dennison.

"Yes, Lady Richfield. That's exactly right. Elly left me shortly after seven this morning. She'd slept in her frock, and wanted to change into a fresh one before rehearsal. She was going to Darry House. What can I do? Shall I come over?"

"There's nothing you can do, Mr. Dennison. Please stay where you are. I'll get back to you as soon as there's any news."

The next call was to her solicitor.

"Yes, Lady Richfield. The papers should be ready in an hour. I have a copy of the will Charles Roundtree drew up before he left for Suez. It stipulates that his estate was to pass to his wife and remain her sole property, even if she were to marry a second time. Upon her death, the estate was to go to their child. Since the child was a girl, she will inherit when she turns twenty-one or marries, in which case the estate will be considered a dowry, in the usual sense."

Isabelle gasped. "If Elly dies before her husband, the estate goes to him."

"Naturally… but you don't think…"

"I don't know what to think. I'm calling Scotland Yard."

She called Scotland Yard and was told, "Sorry ma'am, Chief-Inspector Hayes is out on assignment. He's expected back shortly, can I give him a message?"

"Tell him Lady Richfield needs him on a matter of life and death."

She hung up, phoned Yorkshire, and left messages with Father Tim, and Dr. Vickers.

Isabelle's secretary cancelled all appointments, purchased four first class rail tickets to Bradford, connecting to Skipton, connecting to Settle, and wired for a carriage to be waiting at Settle station and take them to Roundtree's estate. Isabelle checked her watch. It was 12:00. The journey would take about five hours. *We have got to get there in time!*

Chapter Ten

Farmland, North of London, January 5, 1904

"Cor! She finally woke up!"

Elly blinked her eyes. All she could see were shadows. "Who's there? How long have I been asleep?" She heard the click-clack of iron wheels, smelled putrid animal waste, and felt the smooth rhythm of a train speeding along even tracks.

"Gi' me that stuff."

The putrid cloth was on her face again. "No, please, no!" Everything went black.

The train bounced violently and she woke with a start. How long had she been asleep? Where was she? Her empty stomach heaved bitter bile into her mouth and she swallowed it back. Her neck and shoulder screamed with pain. Struggling to find a comfortable position, she realized her wrists were tied behind her back. Thick twine cut into her flesh. Her fingers were numb with cold. She stretched her legs, but her ankles were also bound together. Her eyes adjusted to the darkness and she picked up tiny spots of light shining through cracks in the train carriage walls. The stench of animal waste hung in the stale air.

Tommy Quinn dozed with his back against a wall.

Mick peered down at Elly. "Tommy, she's awake again."

"Bloody hell!" Tommy took the bottle from his pocket and shook it. "It's almost empty. How much did you use on her?" He pushed the soiled cloth and the bottle of chloroform toward Mick.

Elly could already smell the nauseating fumes. "No! Please no! I shall die."

Mick took the bottle and laughed. "I dan' think so Autumn Lydy."

Tommy grabbed Mick's arm. "Wait a minute. If she dies, we don't get paid."

"She ain't gonna die, Tommy, an this'll shut 'er up."

"I'll be quiet as a mouse," Elly spoke softly but distinctly. "See, not a sound." Trembling, she pursed her lips.

The train hit a bump, jerking everyone sideways. The bottle smashed to the floor and Mick screamed, "Bloody 'ell! Tommy, open the bloomin' door, or we'll all get knocked out." Tommy pushed open the wide side door and a fierce, cold wind flooded the train carriage. Elly blinked her eyes against the bright light and loud click-clacking of the wheels. She gulped cold fresh air.

Mick kicked broken glass out the door and shook his head at Tommy. Elly saw a third man sleeping in a far corner. He looked up, and went back to sleep.

Mick held the shaky walls for balance, wobbled to Elly, and leaned his face close to hers. "Mind y' stay nice n' quiet, like y' said, Autumn Lydy, or big Mick's gonna have t' do somfink more t' keep y'quiet." He laughed, " 'ow abou' a kiss for old Mick, for bein' so nice to y'?"

Staring up with terrified eyes, she smelled his foul body odour and turned her face away.

Mick sat down, laughing. The train bounced on.

Physical pain, freezing winds, and mortal fear, pulled Elly in and out of nightmarish sleep. A chariot from hell was dragging her further and further away from people who cared about her. A collage of faces streamed through her tormented dreams: Jeremy O'Connell, Sir John Garingham, Rory Cook, Katherine Stewart, her father, Robert. Where was Robert? Did anyone know she had gone? Surely Isabelle will send someone to look for her. Sam? Where was Sam? He had gone to Settle. Was he already there? Will he find her? Did he know she wasn't in London? Did anyone know? Did anyone care? Writhing in pain, she heard herself cry out.

Mick yelled, "Shut yer gob, y' stupid cow."

"It hurts." She almost longed for the foul smelling cloth. When she was asleep, there had been no pain. "Please untie my hands. It hurts so much." She sobbed uncontrollably. "Please! I can't get away. Please!" Tommy crawled over and untied her hands. She pulled her arms free and lay flat on her back, gasping for breath. Her muscles twitched and her shoulder was on fire. The train car rocked from side-to-side, as huge wheels rolled along the tracks.

Mick sat back laughing. "You're a soddin' milksop, Tommy Quinn. Can't stand t' 'ear a woman cry."

Elly's eyes flew open. Was this the actor Tommy Quinn who owned the brothel -- who ran away with Peg McCarthy on Christmas night?

Mick's gravelly voice droned on. "Me old lady cries reg'lar. Dan' feel right, if I miss a night o' knockin' 'er about. Likes i', she does. Miss 'er I do." He looked at Elly and rubbed himself between the legs. "Ever shagged a woman, Tommy?" He sniggered, "Dan know what yer missin'. I never shagged a real lydy." He stared at Elly's long slender body, stretched across the rough floorboards. "Think they're the same, under their skirts, as regular cows? Or d' they got sonthin' extra?" Still rubbing himself, his body tensed with anticipation. "Wha' say we 'ave a look?"

Heart pounding, Elly curled into a ball. She was suddenly grateful her legs were tied together.

Tommy shivered. "If she's damaged, we won't get paid the balance."

"I di'n' say nothin' bawt damagin'. I just said, 'look.'" As Mick slid toward her, a woman's voice rang out.

"Leave her alone, Mick!"

"Aw, bloody 'ell!" Mick pouted and sat back.

Startled by the strange voice, Elly sat up and leaned against the side of the car. Sickness from a strong narcotic, hunger, thirst, emotional torment, plus an overpowering need to empty her bladder, left her feeling like death would be a blessing.

Suddenly the train jarred and slowed. She braced herself with both hands. Mick looked out the open door. "I see the station." The train slowed, then stopped.

"Go' a take a piss." Mick started to jump out, and Tommy grabbed his arm.

"Me too, but don't let anyone see you, and be quick." The men looked in both directions. The nearly deserted station was on the opposite side of the train.

The men jumped out and Elly yelled, "Me too."

"All right." Tommy came back, untied her ankles, and helped her from the car. "Don't try anything." She saw an enormous tree, miles of railroad tracks, and nothing else but open fields.

Her legs were so weak; she struggled just to stand up. "What could I try?" She staggered toward the tree.

Mick waved his cock, laughing as she wobbled past.

Hiding behind the tree, she relieved herself, then slumped down against the rough bark. She started to rub her burning eyes, caught sight of her filthy gloves, and yanked them off.

The third man stood in the huge open door. As the train whistle blew, his long black hair blew in the wind. Elly gasped. It wasn't a man. It was Peg McCarthy. Elly slumped back, behind the tree. Peg hissed, her enormous dark eyes staring down at Elly. "Come on, you lot, time's a waistin'."

65

Tommy and Mick hurried back to the train. When Elly stayed where she was, Peg shrieked, "Move yer arse!"

Elly jumped with fright. Mick grabbed her and tossed her inside. Tommy closed the huge side door as the train wheels began turning, first slowly, then very fast. Elly crawled into a far corner and curled into a ball. The ride was smooth. They rode in silence. The rhythmic sounds of great iron wheels lulled Elly into a light sleep.

Peg sneered, "You look like 'ell."

Elly's face was chalk-white, under a layer of filth. Her eyes were red and swollen, and her beautiful hair was a tangled mess. Her stockings were ripped and her coat a collage of putrid smears. She glared up. "Do you care?" Her words crackled through parched lips. Her throat constricted painfully.

"Yeah, Oi care. We only been paid 'alf. If y' ain't fit, we dan get the rest. 'ere!" She threw down a small roll of newspaper, and laughed as Elly frantically tore it open. A greasy meat pie was smeared with printer's ink, and Elly devoured it in a few bites. It tasted terrible, but she wished she had another. Peg held a bottle of water just out of Elly's reach. Her eyes filled with desperate tears, and Peg laughed. "Say please, Princess." Furious, Elly lunged at Peg, grabbed the bottle with both hands, and drank it down, all at once. Peg nodded in approval. "Yer all right. I wish Rory could see y' now. Y' look like a filfy beggar." Peg grabbed back the bottle and tossed it into a basket.

Elly felt totally helpless. Peg's insult cut to the core. She did look like a beggar. She was filthy and sick and no one cared. Did anyone even know she was gone? The day was half over. Someone must have noticed.

The others ate their lunch of greasy pies and water.

Tommy handed Peg some money, but she waved it away. "Keep it, Tommy. Oi'll get the rest tonight, from Roundtree. Y' just get yerself to Hull. Y' know Scotland Yard's lookin' fer the blokes what killed that Duchess's nephew. You ain't done the deed, but you was there, so they'll 'ang you along wi' the rest. They dan care about me. Those coppers in Hull only gave y' 'til tonight t' pay 'em off, an' book passage fer us. Oi'll find y' t'morrow, on the boat."

Tommy grabbed her arm. "Come with me, Peg. It's not worth the risk. Roundtree could be lying. If he's got the police waiting…"

"Then *I'll* 'ang. What of it?" Barely taller than a child, she was brave as a warrior.

Tommy shook his head. "You're talking about your life."

"My life? My life's been nothin' but 'ell." She moved closer to him. "This is the first chance Oi've ever 'ad at real money, an' Oi ain't goin' a give it up. If Oi 'ang, Oi'll 'ang poor, but if Oi live, Oi'll live like a lydy, fer the first time, ever."

Clutching his lapels, she gazed into his gray eyes. "What ever folks say about y', Tommy Quinn, yer the only bloke wh' ever treated me decent. If you stay in England, y'll 'ang fer sure, so get the 'ell gone. Oi'm gettin' this money fer us. If Oi dan get t' the boat, go without me. Oi'd rather '*ang* poor, than *live* poor, one day longer. Besides..."

She gritted her teeth and nodded toward Elly. "Oi'll just 'old a knife t' 'er throat till 'er old man pays. Mick'll back me up. Since 'e dan know where the drop off plyce is, 'e go' to do what Oi say. If the coppers do get us, Oi'll get 'er, first."

Tommy clutched her arms. They were thin as sticks. "Just promise you'll be careful."

Not used to kindness, her voice caught in a sob. "Oh, yeah. Oi'll be careful." She switched to her theatrical upper-class accent. "I shall be extremely careful, darling. You may be sure, I am not ready to die."

Amazed by her courage, he grabbed her, kissing her hard.

Pleased, but afraid to show it, she pushed him away. The train slowed. "Get goin', Tommy. Yer train will be here in a few minutes. Oi'll see y' tomorrow."

This time the train slowed, but did not stop. Tommy opened the door just enough to squeeze through. He jumped down, rolling into tall grass beside the tracks. Within seconds the train picked up speed, leaving Tommy far behind.

Peg closed the door and turned back, sneering, "So, Princess. Yer daddy's waitin'."

"Wait, please!" Elly's words flew out all at once. "I know my father's paying you, but I can pay you too, not right now, but I'll have money soon. It's all *my* money actually, if you'll just wait, whatever he's paying you, I'll pay you more... Double." Peg's flaming eyes reminded Elly of the torch she lit at Mrs. Potter's boardinghouse. "Please, Peg... Marguerite, please don't do..."

Peg's cackling laugh made her stop. "So, y' was surprised to see me, Princess. Y' fell right into m' lap, you did. A bleedin' treasure chest, right there in Potter's boardin' 'ouse." She carefully slid down to the floor, across from her. Mick stretched out with his head in Peg's lap. She stroked his grimy hair and whispered in her witch's voice. "Wiv' the money yer farver's payin', Tommy and me can get clean out a England, and live nice, fer a long time. Can y' believe it Mick? This stupid cow ran away from money." Mick reached a huge hand and squeezed Peg's breast. She slapped his hand and he laughed.

Elly sighed wearily. "How did you find out about me?"

"I din' know nothin' at first. Then, there was this bloke snoopin' around, down by the docks, askin' about some rich girl, run away, supposed t' 'ave crossed the channel. Said she were tall, thin, wiv red 'air, funny name: somthin' Round - Tree. This bloke said he were a private investigator workin' fer the girl's farver. 'alf the girl's in England's tall, thin, wiv red 'air. Din't give it a second thought. Then one day I was doin' Bates, an' 'e..."

Elly's mouth dropped open. "You were still with Eric Bates after he..."

"'e paid me good money, y' stupid cow. Oi'd do things. Things he couldn't ask 'is lydy wife t' do. Not really bad things, mind. Not like other blokes Oi done, but bad enough 'is wife would a divorced 'im." She hissed a laugh, making Elly shudder. "One day, after Oi done 'im, 'e was talking sloppy, the way men does after..." She snickered. "He was mad at O'Connell fer keepin' y'. You was a runaway. 'e din' remember yer first name, but he remembered Round - Tree, 'cause 'e an' O'Connell 'ad a laugh over it."

Elly pulled up her knees and lowered her head.

"Oi went back to this investigator bloke an' made me a deal. First Oi 'ad t' make sure you was the right girl. Oi wasn't gonna grab some cow off the street, drag 'er 'alf way across the country and not get paid. There was no picture of you, nowhere. 'ow come?"

Elly shook her head.

"Rich people always 'ave pictures a' their brats."

"My father never liked me."

"Bli'me! You must 'a' been a rotter. The only picture anyone knew about, was a paintin' yer teacher done at school. Yer farver learned about i' when 'e went there lookin' fer y'. The picture was in London already, so Oi made Tommy take a job in the gallery." She mussed Mick's hair. "First regular day's work Tommy ever done, Oi wager."

Mick laughed, "And 'e 'ope's it's 'is last."

Peg hissed, "'e din't have to work that stinkin' job two days. Yer picture got 'ung on the wall and you walked through the door."

Mick chortled, "Like a lamb to the slaughter." They laughed raucously. Mick wrestled Peg to the floor and lay on top of her.

The train bounced and he rolled off Peg, over to Elly. He put his hand on her ankle and slid his fingers up her leg. She kicked out, catching him in the chest. His huge hand swung back, savagely struck her face, and knocked her to the floor.

Peg leapt on top of Mick and held a knife to his throat. The train jerked and the knife drew blood. Terrified, Elly wished Peg would drive the blade deeper. Peg kept the knife where it was and spoke through clenched teeth. "We need that money, Mick. If she's damaged, we dan get it. If you bugger this, Oi'll kill you. Get it?"

Mick put a hand on his throat. Blood ran over his fingers. "Yeah," he sulked. "Oi get it."

Peg moved off him, sat back, but kept the knife ready.

Elly lay on the floor, a welt rising on her throbbing temple.

Chapter Eleven

London the same day

"I need to see Chief-Inspector Hayes immediately." It was 2:30 when Lady Richfield stormed past a middle-aged sergeant and a young duty officer at the front desk of Scotland Yard. Her solicitor, Roger Foxhall, followed with short quick steps.

The startled officer chased after them. "I'm sorry, madam." The hard soles of his boots banged loudly. "...but the Chief-Inspector's gone to Whitechapel, there's been a double murder."

"Well, young man," she spun around, boring into him with fierce blue eyes. "I'm trying to prevent a third murder. If he's not back yet, show me to his junior. Somebody – anybody-- who can escort me to Yorkshire. Now!"

The officer trembled. "May I ask who's requiring assistance?"

"Lady Richfield."

"Yes, ma'am, right away, ma'am, sorry for the inconvenience." He ran down the hall.

Isabelle turned to Foxhall. "Damn these delays. Hayes was supposed to be back long before now."

Foxhall anxiously twisted the brim of his hat. "For my part, I am so terribly sorry. The papers should have taken half-the-time to copy. That new clerk of mine, the one who spilled the ink, he'll be discharged, I promise you."

"Don't be absurd." She waved her hand. "The poor boy was frightened out of his wits. He won't do it again." She paced the floor. "As it turns out, we could have taken our time." She stared down the hall. "Damn! What's keeping the man?"

"Lady Richfield." The young officer raced back. "Inspector Doddington will see you now." He made a lopsided bow and returned to the front desk.

A middle-aged man in a well tailored suit followed the officer down the hall. He politely inclined his head. "Lady Richfield?" He shook her hand.

"Good afternoon Inspector, thank you for seeing us. This is my solicitor, Roger Foxhall."

He shook Foxhall's hand. "How-do-you-do, sir. I'm Inspector Doddington. Please be so kind as to follow me." He led them down the hall, toward his office. "Will you take tea, Lady Richfield?"

She clenched her jaw. "No - thank - you. This is not a social call."

"Quite so." Opening the door of his small, plain office, the Inspector allowed Isabelle and Foxhall to enter first. They passed two rows of filing cabinets and sat down on hardwood chairs. The Inspector squeezed past them and sat behind his desk. "So, how may I help you?"

Isabelle started to speak and Foxhall politely interrupted, "If you will allow me, M' Lady." Clearly and precisely, Foxhall told the history of the Roundtree family, emphasizing the roles of the men, producing documents, and winning the inspector's interest. At first, Isabelle was annoyed Foxhall had taken charge. Quickly understanding his slant on the story and watching the inspector's interest grow, she kept silent. As always, a young man's misfortune was of great concern. A young woman's misfortune was merely coincidental.

When Foxhall finished, the Inspector paused, drumming his fingers on the desktop. "Mr. Foxhall, how do you know that the young lady was abducted?"

Isabelle's mouth dropped open. "He just told you..."

"I beg your pardon, Madam, but the gentleman has given me a good deal of background. He has given me no proof that Miss Roundtree has not simply run off. Since she has a history of running away, how can you be sure she hasn't done it again?"

Isabelle was stunned. "I just know that she hasn't. She has just started working at the theatre. Her young man came to town, only yesterday. All of her friends..."

The Inspector stood up. "I'm sorry Lady Richfield, but we have a good many officers out on cases, just now. When the Chief-Inspector returns, he will decide how we can best assist you. If you'll follow me, we have a rather comfortable waiting area. It's just this way." Before Isabelle could object, the Inspector was out the door, leading the way down a different corridor.

It was another hour before Chief-Inspector Hayes and his sergeant arrived back at Scotland Yard. Tired and out of sorts, they dragged themselves into the station. Dying for a meal and a rest, Hayes was livid when the duty officer told him a lady and her solicitor were waiting for him. Keeping his temper, he strode to the waiting room door. When he saw

Isabelle through the glass, his eyes opened wide. He hurried inside. "Lady Richfield?"

Isabelle skipped polite preliminaries. "Chief-Inspector, you may remember a young lady you met at my house, Christmas Eve. Her name is Elly Fielding, and she's in terrible danger. I fear for her life."

It was 4:00 p.m. when Isabelle, the Chief-Inspector, and his Sergeant boarded the train at St. Pancras Station on their way to Bradford, to change for Skipton, to change for Settle. Arrival time was 9:06 p.m. The local constable had been wired orders to escort them from the station, to the Roundtree Estate.

*

At 4:30, rehearsal finished. Jeremy, Katherine, Evan, and Michael Burns were on their way to Gildstein Gallery. Rory came out of the stage door and Jeremy called, "Mr. Cook, why don't you join us? We are going to view Robert Dennison's exhibition."

Rory gritted his teeth, whispering, "Why in hell would I want to do that?"

Jeremy whispered back, "Because you cannot fight a competitor you do not know."

"Why should I even bother? Elly might be married and on her way out of the country by now." He was close to tears.

"And she may have escaped and be making her way back to us."

"And if she does come back, what then? She's already given herself to Dennison."

Jeremy burst out laughing. "'Given herself'? Good Lord, Rory, you sound like an old spinster lady at a church supper. Are you still in love with the first woman you ever -- gave yourself to?"

Rory rolled his eyes. "Of course I'm not. How absurd. But a woman's sensibilities are not the same as a man's. Everyone knows that."

"Really?" He moved closer. "And what of Isabelle's 'sensibilities'? Is she ready to leave her husband because of a pleasant tumble with you?"

Nearly falling over with shock, Rory mumbled, "Lady Richfield is a mature woman. She knows her own mind."

"And Elly does not know her own mind. I quite agree with you. She is barely more than a child. She may stay in love with her art-master, or she may not. She may tire of him and look for other companionship, and there you will be, ready and waiting. I suggest you meet this fellow and see what he is all about. At the very least, you should see this portrait she has spoken of."

They all climbed into a cab and rode to South Kensington, Exhibition Road, and the gallery entrance. A placard read:

Premier Exhibition:
ROBERT DENNISON
Oils and Pastels
January 5th - 10th

Just past a small reception area, they stopped and stared at a sumptuous vision: *Autumn Lady*. Katherine caught her breath. Rory gasped. His shoulders tensed to his ears. Evan tilted his head like a dog hearing a strange sound. "Daddy, is that Elly?"

Jeremy cleared his throat, "Well - um, yes - Evan. That is an artist's interpretation of Elly, the way she might look in a few years' time. Not quite the girl we know, eh? Do you like the way he has painted the red of her hair, so it blends with the red and yellow of the leaves?"

Evan moved his head from side to side. "Is she standing up or lying down?"

Jeremy shrugged. "I believe that is for the viewer to decide. What is your opinion?"

Even walked close to the painting. "I think she's lying down."

Rory moved close to Jeremy, gritting his teeth and whispering, "Did she model for him in bed?"

Jeremy whispered back, "I'm sure he would have wished it. Since they were at a very proper school, and our girl is incapable of projecting that sort of sensuality, we must assume the artist has a powerful imagination."

Rory nodded. "I see what you mean -- know thine enemy."

Jeremy laughed quietly.

Their reverie broke when women laughed in the main gallery. Jeremy, Katherine, and Michael followed the voices and walked inside. An elderly man hurried past, followed by a harried labourer.

Robert Dennison stood conversing with a group of elegant ladies. Several men studied the paintings, scribbled notes, and made sketches on wide pads. Robert saw Michael, excused himself, and hurried over. Michael made the introductions, and Robert shook hands all around. "I'm so pleased to meet you all. Is there any news from Lady Richfield?"

73

Katherine shook her head. "It's too soon. Mr. Dennison. She will not have reached Yorkshire, yet."

Robert looked very worried. "Yes, of course. I've lost all concept of time."

Jeremy called to Rory and Evan, still staring at *Autumn Lady*. "Evan, Mr. Cook, come and meet Mr. Dennison." Jeremy smiled to himself. Robert Dennison was tall and slim, with soft brown eyes and long brown hair. He must have his pick of women, not just schoolgirls.

Rory clenched his jaw, forced a civil expression, and trudged over. He tried appearing taller, by looking Robert in the eye without raising his chin. Robert extended his hand, smiling warmly. "So you're Rory Cook. Elly is terribly fond of you. She's told me what an excellent friend you have been. Thank you so much." Rory accepted Robert's hand, nodded, but said nothing.

Evan jabbed his small hand into Robert's. "I like the picture of Elly, even though it doesn't look like her."

Jeremy felt embarrassed, but Robert laughed as he shook Evan's small hand. "Thanks Evan. I don't think it looks very like her, either. I prefer the real girl, don't you?"

Evan smiled back. "Yes, I do."

The elderly man called, "Mr. Dennison!" Robert excused himself, hurried out of sight.

The actors viewed Robert's other paintings and pastels. There were picturesque landscapes, voluptuous nudes, and a series of small field animals. Rory lingered by three paintings of beautiful old stone buildings.

Jeremy joined him and read a title: "*Heathhead School, Yorkshire*. So, this is where they met. Dennison must have been happy there to make it look so inviting."

Rory scowled. "Of course it's lovely. That's where he found Elly."

Evan pulled Jeremy to a small canvas with a delightfully fuzzy squirrel holding an acorn. "Daddy, can I have this one?"

Jeremy studied the painting. It made him smile. "Yes, I think this would be very nice in your upstairs room. Katie, what do you think?"

She agreed and he was about to make the purchase, when Robert returned, breathless and perspiring. "Please, Mr. O'Connell, allow me to paint Evan a copy, as a gift. You have been so kind, I can't have you *buying* my painting."

74

"Nonsense, we all like it, and fortunately I can well afford it. You appear to be out of breath."

Robert shook his head. "Mr. Gildstein's in a pickle. He needs three men to load and unload. Day-before-yesterday, two of his regular blokes took sick and sent replacements. Today, those replacements didn't show, so I was helping load the last artist's crates onto a cart."

"Just a moment." Jeremy's thoughts raced. "Two new chaps worked here yesterday and the day before."

"Yes, and they weren't much good. Today they didn't even…"

"They didn't show up at all?"

"No, why?" He looked worried.

"They saw Elly and *Autumn Lady* together?"

"Yes, of course they did, why? Do you…?"

"And today both the men and Elly are missing. What did they look like? Can you describe them?"

Robert wiped sweat off his brow as he concentrated. "Well yes, one was a big fellow, very strong with dark hair. They called him, Mick. The other was a small, wiry chap called Jake. He was quite a bit older, with a thick thatch of yellow hair and a nasty expression. He wasn't very fit and couldn't lift anything heavy. One of his teeth was missing."

"Which one?" Jeremy's heart pounded.

"Umm," Robert struggled to remember, "I believe it was this one." He touched an upper tooth.

Jeremy felt faint. Fighting for breath, he whispered, "Mick may be Mick Tanner, a butcher's assistant and would-be actor. The other was probably an actor in a wig, named Tommy Quinn."

Chapter Twelve

Town of Settle, Yorkshire, the same day

Rex's rope tore from Sam's hand, jerking him awake. The dog raced from the pavilion, toward the house, barking madly.

"REX! HEEL! REX!" Sam chased raggedly after the dog and found himself at the main entrance. A small group of people stood around a neat carriage. Sweat shone on the horses' quivering backs, and mist puffed from their nostrils into the damp night air. Sam moved closer and froze. Elly was on the ground, clutching Rex. Her eyes were red and swollen. Her face was streaked with dirt and an ugly bruise spread across one side of her face. Her hair hung in ugly clumps and her clothes were torn. She saw Sam, gasped, and quickly looked away.

A well-dressed elderly man yelled, "Someone get rid of that damn dog." A servant reached for Rex, and the dog snapped savagely. The man pulled a revolver from his belt. "The dog's mad. Move aside Elisa."

"No, father!" Elly clung to Rex and the dog growled, preparing to spring at Anthony Roundtree.

"Rex, HEEL!" Rex ran to Sam and sat panting. Sam grabbed the rope around Rex's neck and forced a laugh, "Sorry, sir. My dog's going to entertain your guests tomorrow. He's a great dog, just *loves* the ladies. Sorry to bother you, Miss." Sam and Rex sped into the woods.

As soon as they were out of sight, they stopped for breath. Rex looked up at Sam. His wet tongue hung out the side of his mouth. "You found her, Rex. Good dog!" He scratched Rex's head. "That bastard Roundtree has a gun. This changes everything. How are we going to get her past a bullet?"

He led Rex back behind the house. Now Elly's windows were brightly lit. Standing below, in the damp woods, Sam helplessly watched the upstairs windows. Elly and her aunt passed to and fro. He wanted to charge up the stairs and save her, but her father had that gun.

*

Upstairs in Elly's room, Lillian removed her niece's ruined coat, pushed her into a chair, and looked at her face. Two maids came up the stairs. One carried a basin of steaming water, towels, and soap, the other a tray of food.

Lillian directed them. "Sarah, put the food over there. Mary, bring the basin over here. Thank you girls. That will be all." They smiled nervously at Elly, curtsied, and left. Lillian locked the door and put the key in her pocket. Elly watched the key, wondering how she could get it. Lillian looked at her niece. "Elisa, dear, you were expected hours ago. Sir John will be here soon and we must get you ready. What an ugly bruise. He won't like that. I'll cover it with powder."

"Why will he care? He's been bruising me for years."

"Never on your face, dear. He never marked your face."

"Does it matter where?"

"Hush child!"

Elly forced herself to sit still as her aunt soaked a cloth and cleaned her hands and face. She cringed as the cloth rubbed painfully over the bruise.

Lillian studied her face. "It's not that bad, dear. I've had far worse."

Elly sighed, "Of course you have Aunt, but you're forever falling down stairs."

The older woman spoke without emotion. "I've never fallen down stairs in my entire life."

"Oh please, Auntie! Every time I come home from school, you have new bruises. Let me have that food, I'm famished." She pushed her aunt aside and pulled her chair to the desk. After two bites, her stomach cramped painfully. She pushed the plate away. Suddenly dizzy, she put her head in her hands.

Lillian gently shook her. "Not now, dear. You'll have time enough to rest on the train. Sit up. I need to dress your hair."

She was suddenly wide awake. "What train?"

"You're being married in an hour. Then, you and Sir John are taking the train to Hull, and sailing for Rotterdam at midnight."

"NO!" Elly was on her feet, racing toward the door. She yanked the knob. It held firm. Turning back, she stared around the room like a caged animal. There was no other way out, the windows were sealed. She stopped. The window glass rattled in the wind. How was that possible? Looking carefully, she could see small holes where the nails had been removed. Sam had been here. Her heart slowed.

Lillian picked up a hair brush. "Come dear, we have to get you out of that soiled frock and into the wedding gown."

Elly clutched the door knob. "No! No wedding gown, Aunt. That's nonsense."

"To you perhaps, but not to me. I have been dreaming of your wedding for years, and I am going to see you married in that gown." Tears welled in her eyes. "It's the only dream I have left."

"For God's sake Aunt, you have dreams enough for the entire continent." A wave of nausea took over and she slumped across the bed. Her head pounded and her body ached.

Lillian wrung her hands, staring at the wedding gown. "If I'd had a dowry, I could have had a husband and a gown of my own."

Elly buried her face in the bedclothes. "Is that what marriage is to you? A gown? Take the gown."

Lillian watched the girl, then sighed. "You're not yourself, dearest. We won't talk further. Come, let's get you ready."

"No please, Aunt Lillian." Elly forced herself to sit up. If she could keep her aunt talking, she would forget what she was supposed to do. "I'm sorry, Auntie. Please tell me your dreams." She held out her hand. "I want to hear them, really." Her eyes burned and she swallowed down a sour taste in her mouth.

Lillian sighed sadly, sat next to Elly, and took her hand. A faraway look came over her wrinkled face.

Elly needed to get the key from Lillian's pocket. She forced herself to speak lovingly. "I know you wanted to get married."

"Dear child, I shouldn't bother you with my sorrows, but yes, of course I wanted to get married. When I was young, before Mama died, quite a few beaux came courting." She smiled at the memory.

The key was on her other side. Elly's arm slid around her Aunt's waist in a pretend embrace.

"I was pretty then, like you." She touched Elly's cheek. "Even after Mama… while Papa was still alive, I thought it was possible. I'd taken over running the house, but it was nothing a good housekeeper couldn't have done, and Papa was so handsome. I hoped he'd marry again. Lots of ladies set their caps for him." She smiled and suddenly seemed younger. "They used to call on the slimmest excuses. We children used to laugh so."

Elly's arm could not reach Lillian's pocket.

Lillian took a deep breath. "After Papa's accident, Charlie went to Germany to study engineering, and I was left alone with Tony. He'd always been a bully, even as a child. I kept hoping he'd grow out of it, but with no one to curb his temper, it grew worse. We lived pleasantly enough, until one day, a gentleman I'd been keeping company with, proposed marriage. Tony told him there was no dowry. None. The family fortune was gone. The man made his excuses and I never saw him again."

Elly had heard this story many times, but pretended to be surprised. "That's horrid! How could he treat you like that?"

Lillian laughed sadly, "Which one do you mean? The gentleman, or my brother? I was a grown woman by then, without a penny to call my own. I knew then that I'd never marry, and I'd be dependent on Tony forever. On top of it all, he said there was a chance we'd lose the estate. Then…" She smiled, clasping her hands. "A telegram arrived from Charlie. He'd married a German girl, Bertha, and she was expecting a child. Her father's firm had bought shares in the Suez Canal and Charlie, his father in-law and mother in-law were traveling there. Bertha was coming to us for her confinement."

Elly's insides felt hollow. It was all true. She was Charles Roundtree's daughter.

Lillian glowed from the happy memory. "My darling Charlie's wife came to us. She was beautiful and very sweet. She spoke quite good English and we got on very well. Tony disliked her, but he dislikes all women." Her brows creased. "Poor Bertha's labor was very difficult…" Her face hardened. "Enough storytelling." She stood up and walked toward the wedding dress.

Suddenly weakening, Elly wanted to cry. "Aunt Lillian, please don't make me do this."

"I haven't the power to make anyone do anything."

Elly dove for her aunt's pocket. "Then, give me the key. Please!"

With lightning speed, Lillian took the key from her pocket and dropped it down her bodice. Elly lunged for it, then stopped, as good manners held her back.

Lillian smiled. "I'll give you the key, dearest." Seeming to look past Elly, her glassy eyes focused on something far away. "But first, I'm going to see you as a bride." With one hand Lillian picked up a hair brush. With the other, she grabbed Elly's hair, dragging her backwards into a chair. The girl screamed with pain and stumbled as she slid onto the seat. Lillian removed the few remaining hairpins and pulled the brush through the tangled mass. She had to pull hard and Elly screamed again.

Lillian ignored her cries and kept brushing. "We are women, Elisa. We have no power to do anything, ever. Men are cruel and we are here for their pleasure." She brushed so hard, Elly nearly fell backwards.

She yanked her head forward and stood to face her aunt. "That's not true, really it's not. I've been in London with marvellously strong women who do as they please, and brilliant men who love women, and know how to be gentle..."

Lillian grabbed Elly's shoulders. "Don't ever let John Garingham hear you talk like that. He'll beat you bloody, I swear he will."

Elly lurched back, her eyes were enormous.

Lillian trembled. "He and Tony are two of a kind. They believe women are here for only one purpose. When their women don't behave, they're punished." Suddenly, Lillian laughed a high pitched, childish giggle. Her face spread into a vapid grin and she tunelessly sang:

"When a merry maiden marries,
Sorrow goes and pleasure tarries...."

She skipped to the dresser and returned with a dozen dead roses, tied with a crisp white-satin ribbon. She curtsied, presenting them to her niece. Horrified, Elly stared at the gruesome bouquet and her Aunt's demented smile. A draught rattled the loose window panes and Elly looked again. Where was Sam?

The door handle shook, but the lock held. Anthony Roundtree shouted, "Open this damn door, Lillian. Sir John and the vicar are here."

Lillian woke from her demented trance and looked at the dead flowers in her hand. Confused, she laid them aside. "Ten minutes – Please! The child just arrived. We're still dressing." Lillian leapt at Elly and practically ripped off her soiled frock. Elly stood frozen as Lillian bound her into an unbelievably stiff corset. She pushed Elly against the bedstead. "Exhale, now -- more!" Lillian pulled the laces tighter-and-tighter.

Elly started to lose consciousness and Lillian passed a vial of smelling salts under her nose. Her head jerked up and tears flooded her eyes. Lillian screamed, "Don't cry! For God's sake, DON'T CRY!" Elly was so startled, the tears vanished. Lillian tossed a wide hooped crinoline over Elly's head, and over that, the white gown, with yards of lace and heavy satin. Lillian pushed dozens of tiny buttons through fine loops of thread, closing the back, high neck, and long sleeves.

Elly stepped into white satin slippers and wanted to die. "This dress is my coffin." She closed her eyes as the veil was secured to her head.

Lillian sighed. "We didn't have time to dress your hair, dear. You'll have to wear it long, like Juliet."

JULIET! Visions of everyone she had left in London flooded her mind - Jeremy O'Connell, Katherine Stewart, Lady Richfield, Robert, Rory, Lester... She felt a surge of power. *NO!*

Lillian looked Elly up and down and nodded in approval. "You look as beautiful as I expected." She took the key from her bodice and unlocked the door.

Three men stood in the hall. Anthony Roundtree and Sir John Garingham stopped their conversation. Lillian shuddered and scurried into a corner, behind the dolls' house.

Father Folen hesitated, then shuffled past the other men, into the room. Elly ran to greet him. "It's been so long, Father Folen." She hugged him, whispering, "For the love of Mary, don't do to me what you did to my mother."

The blood drained from his face as he called, "Mr. Roundtree, I cannot perform a wedding ceremony at this time, in this room. It is not sacred ground, or a permissible hour."

Roundtree smirked as he locked the door and put the key in his pocket. "My chapel is still at the side of the house, where it was eighteen years ago. It was close enough then, and it still is. Write down whatever time of day your Bishop will approve, and have done with it. No one will know the difference."

Father Folen glanced guiltily at Elly then stepped away. Elly was suddenly facing Anthony Roundtree and Sir John Garingham.

Sir John offered his hand. She froze, losing her breath, trying desperately not to cry. His lips formed a smile but his eyes were cold. "You sent your father on quite a chase, my dear. He even had an investigator scouring Paris. That cost him a good deal of money."

She clenched her teeth. "It's my money."

Sir John's expression hardened. His hands became fists at his sides.

Roundtree stormed toward her and she ran backwards, tripping over her train and falling to the floor. Her skirt flew up like a tent and she struggled to hold it down. He leaned over her. "What the bloody hell are you talking about? Your money? You filthy little bastard." Her hooped petticoat was like a wild monster with a life of its own. Roundtree screamed, "You should be grateful you've had a roof over your head all these years. Instead you've caused nothing but trouble."

"I'm not a bastard." Elly flattened the hoops. "My mother was married to Charles Roundtree."

Anthony Roundtree seized her arm and dragged her up off the floor. She cried out in pain, as he yelled into her face, "Your whore of a mother got herself with child before she was married. Her parents were more interested in money than their daughter, so they went off to Egypt and shipped the bitch here, to drop her brat. They all died and I was left with you."

"And my money."

He threw her against the wall. She crashed against the bookcase and reeled back, nearly losing her balance.

Roundtree turned to the priest. "Come along, Father. Let's get my daughter married. They've got a train to catch."

Father Folen's hands were shaking. He dropped his briefcase. Papers scattered. Roundtree's quick eye found the marriage license. Seizing it, he hurried to the school desk near the window, pushed the tray of food aside, dipped the pen in the inkwell, and offered it to Sir John. "Your pleasure, sir."

The bridegroom smiled and signed the certificate.

Roundtree called, "Elisa, sign this."

Overcome with nausea, unable to breathe, she leaned against the bookcase. Wind and rain rattled the loose window glass.

"Sign this!" Roundtree grabbed her arm and dragged her to the desk. He forced the pen into her hand and twisted her wrist toward the paper. She screamed with pain.

Sir John held up his hand, asking for silence. "A word in your ear, my dear." Smiling with eyes-of-ice, he offered Elly his arm.

Paralyzing terror overcame her. His large hand was like a vice around her thin arm, as he pulled her across the floor. Easing her into a corner, he turned his back to the rest of the room, put his hands on the wall on either side of her face, and leaned in. Her hoops were crushed between his legs and the wall behind.

Their faces were so close she could see deep pores in his oily skin and smell his breath, sour from cigars and bad teeth. His raspy whisper made her shudder. His fake smile was more threatening than Roundtree's bellowing.

He spoke very slowly. "You are making this very hard on yourself, my dear. Surely you know that it is inevitable. You - will - be - my - wife."

Her legs buckled. He grabbed her around the waist, holding her tight against him. His mouth pressed her ear. "Now, my dear…" She felt his hot breath against her skin. "I want you to listen very carefully, because what I am going to say will affect the next several years of your life."

Her stomach lurched.

Garingham's quiet rasp continued. "Your life can be very pleasant. You can have all the luxuries money can buy: houses, cars, servants, clothes, horses. You can travel, go to the theatre, give parties, entertain…"

She looked surprised and his smile broadened.

"Yes, you can even entertain your new friends: the London thespians, even that foolish painter, anyone at all."

She waited, terrified to hear the conditions.

"All you have to do is obey me, absolutely."

Absolutely? He had nearly broken her wrist when she refused to kiss him. Aunt Lillian just said that he would beat her bloody. She gasped, whispering, "What do I have to do?"

"Good, good. That's better." He let her go and she collapsed against the bookcase. He looked her in the eye, grinning with yellow teeth. "My demands will be no different from those of any husband's. You must be the lady of my house, a hostess to my guests, cheer me when I am gloomy, allow me privacy when I require it, show respect and affection at all times, be always genteel, always agreeable, never contradict, never be cross or shrewish, and above all - never cry. I cannot abide a woman who cries. Since you are so fond of playing and singing, you may entertain me and my guests."

He stopped. His lips pulled into a tight smile. "Your most important commission will be to give me sons, while of course, servicing my needs in the bedroom. I will not be one of those husbands who visits his wife's boudoir, once a week, with the lights off. Even to experienced women, my pleasures seem somewhat… unusual. Knowing you as well as I do, I expect you will resist me. You have a strong will. Breaking it will be a challenge and a pleasure."

She started to cry and held her breath to stop it.

"Good, good! You do know how to obey." His harsh whisper became even softer. "You must never cry."

The spasms of her sobs' were driven inward and her chest heaved soundlessly.

"We will have a vast fortune, my dear." Her eyes went wide and he smiled. "As you so aptly pointed out, it is *your* money, but it will soon be mine. You will need a manager, in any event. Women are incapable of managing their own affairs."

Elly's chest heaved. If she could not release her tears, she would explode.

"But what is the good of money, if a man has no sons to spend it on, hmm?"

She shuddered.

"I am no longer a young man, and I have a strong desire to have sons. So, you must give me sons."

Her cheeks burned. Her corset stays pierced like knives.

"I want three, at least. Do you understand?"

She nodded, clenching her teeth.

"Good! After you have given me three sons, if we are not totally happy with one another, we may come to an arrangement. We may even live apart." She looked up quickly and he laughed. "I see *that* idea appeals to you. Do you dislike me so much, then?"

She lowered her eyes.

He laughed again. "No matter." He walked back, toward Roundtree.

Heart racing, she frantically calculated. *I could have three sons in three years, and be rid of him, forever. Or I might have daughters. What if I can't conceive at all?* She whispered, "Sir John?"

He turned to see her trembling. "Yes, my dear?"

Her body heaved like a locomotive. "What if…"

"Yes?"

"What if I cannot do all that you require?" The tears poured out, as her head fell back against the wall.

His eyes narrowed. "Then, I must teach you how to obey me. And while you are learning, you will give me sons."

"And, if I cannot give you sons?"

He shrugged casually. "Well, if you are not capable of performing you marital duties, you will have to be replaced. Once your estate belongs to me, little else matters. It would be a shame if a young, beautiful woman, like yourself, was to meet with a tragic accident, but such things happen every day." Turning away, he stepped past Roundtree, leaned against a windowsill, crossed his arms, and smiled. "Eighteen-years-ago, Charles Roundtree met with a tragic accident. It was childishly simple for me to arrange."

She stared at him.

"And now, my dear. Your father is waiting. Come sign the paper."

As if in a trance, she crossed the room, signed the paper, dropped the pen on the floor, and walked toward the dolls' house where her aunt was standing. The two women watched in silence as Roundtree retrieved the pen and pointed it at the priest. "Sign this!"

Father Folen, white faced and shaking, looked at Elly. She was pale as a corpse.

Roundtree roared, "None of your games, priest. Sign!"

Father Folen shook his head. "I won't do it. Not again. I sinned, unlawfully marrying you to this child's mother."

Roundtree took out his revolver and aimed it at the priest. "I was afraid you might turn righteous one day." He cocked the gun and put his finger on the trigger.

"You can kill me, sir. I won't do it."

Still looking at the priest, Roundtree walked to his cowering sister. "Oh, but I won't kill *you*." He put an arm around Lillian and pointed the gun at her head. She closed her eyes and held her breath. Roundtree smirked, "What do you say now, Reverend? Now will you sign?"

Father Folen held up his hands. "Move the gun away from the lady, sir. Please!"

"First, sign!"

There was frantic knocking on the door.

Roundtree bellowed, "Go away!"

A frightened voice called, "Pardon me, sir, but there are detectives from Scotland Yard downstairs. They say the matter is urgent."

Roundtree froze. His eyes were wild. He yelled back, "Sir John's car is out front. Tell the driver to bring it around the back and keep the motor running. I'll be down directly."

Without warning, Father Folen flew at Roundtree, pushing Lillian out of the way. With a deafening explosion, the gun went off. Elly pulled up her hoopskirt, ran across the room, and hurled herself against Sir John, driving him against the window, through the shattering glass. He howled, plunging down toward the hard ground below. His feet flew up and one boot caught in a hoop of Elly's skirt, pulling her through the window after him.

Chapter Thirteen

Outside, looking up into the bedroom, Sam ran back from a hail of shattered glass. The car drove around the house, shining bright headlights, illuminating the area. The driver swerved, then stopped violently as Garingham flew through the window like a great bat. His frock coat blew open, as his arms and legs splayed in four directions. The illusion of wings did nothing to slow his back dive, head first into the hard ground.

Sam yelled, "NO!" as the white mass of Elly's gown sailed after him. Garingham hit the ground with a terrible crunching sound and lay still. Dark blood gushed over the moist earth, surrounding his head like a gruesome halo.

Elly stopped in mid-air. Sam blinked his eyes. In uneven beams from the car headlights, she looked like a ghost hovering. For a split second, he wondered if the shot had killed her, and he was watching her soul ascend to a higher plane. He ran up to the house and saw that her gown had caught on the trellis. She hung almost upside down, desperately trying to free herself. Her corset kept her from bending at the waist and reaching the hoop, caught above.

Sam made a running jump up the trellis. Grabbing hold, he forced the toes of his boots through the thick rose canes. He strained, making his way up, until he was beside Elly. With one arm, he seized the captive hoop, and pulled on it with his full weight. Her gown ripped free as the entire trellis gave way, crashing them both to the ground. Sam landed on his back with Elly and the trellis on top of him. He moaned with pain.

Anthony Roundtree had dropped the gun, unlocked the bedroom door, dashed down the backstairs, and outside, past Sam and Elly.

Sam lifted his chin. "REX! AFTER HIM!" The howling dog lunged after Roundtree. The man's eyes were wild with fear. Rex leapt from behind and knocked him face down onto the muddy grass. Roundtree twisted into a terrified ball, as Rex's vicious teeth kept him prisoner.

Upstairs, Father Folen lay in a pool of blood, a bullet in his neck. Lillian Roundtree knelt beside him, sobbing.

The gunshot had sent Chief-Inspector Hayes, his sergeant, and several servants racing up the front stairs. The Chief-Inspector reached the

86

bedroom and stared at the priest's bloody body. "Call a doctor!" A servant sped out the door.

Lillian cried, "Tony killed him. Tony shot Father Folen."

The Chief-inspector sped to the shattered window, looked down, and saw Roundtree attacked by a large dog. He ran back out, past the body. "How do I get outside?"

"This way, sir." A servant led him down the backstairs and around the side of the house. The dog held Roundtree captive. When Rex saw the officers, he stopped barking, but stayed in position, teeth bared, haunches tense, ready to spring.

The sergeant slowly approached. "Easy boy. Good dog."

Gasping painfully, Sam called, "REX! COME! GOOD BOY!" Whining frantically, Rex ran circles around the pile of rubble containing Elly and Sam.

The sergeant pulled Roundtree to his feet. The Chief-Inspector yanked his arms behind his back and clamped handcuffs around his wrists. "Anthony Roundtree: I'm arresting you for embezzlement, and the murder of a priest."

A host of servants carefully pulled Elly and Sam from the thorny rose-canes, fishing line, dress hoops, and the trellis.

*

Within the hour, Doctor Frederick Vickers was seeing to their wounds. He gave Sam an injection of morphine and went to check on Elly. She was stretched out on the drawing room sofa, wrapped in a soft dressing gown. Pillows were under her head and a blanket over her legs. Her skin was ashen and her breathing shallow. The shredded wedding dress, bent skirt hoops, and corset stays were piled on the floor.

Isabelle watched as the doctor examined Elly's injuries.

Relieved, he smiled and nodded. "Miss Roundtree, you are a very lucky young lady. You've got some nasty bruises and your ankle is badly sprained. You'll need to stay off that for at least a fortnight." He chuckled softly. "I believe corsets to be the most ungodly garments ever created, but that one did you good. It held you together and may have saved your life. You'll feel very sore for the next few days. Tomorrow you'll feel worse that you do right now. Just remember," he shook his finger, "stay off that ankle." A servant brought her a cup of hot soup. The doctor gave Elly a comforting pat on the hand, nodded respectfully to Isabelle, and went downstairs to check on Sam.

Lethargic from the morphine, Sam lay on a kitchen table, quietly moaning. His right arm was stretched at an odd angle.

Isabelle followed Dr. Vickers, and watched as he gently probed Sam's chest.

"Mr. Smelling, your right arm has a bad break. At least two ribs are cracked, and there may be internal injuries as well. I'm going to set that arm, and it's going to hurt. The morphine will help, but you'll feel this, so I apologize in advance."

Without further warning, the doctor snapped Sam's bone into place. Sam screamed, then slumped back, unconscious. Isabelle raced to his left side and gently stroked his forehead. The doctor poured dry plaster into a basin of water. In seconds, he began forming a cast around Sam's right arm.

Sam moaned softly, and Isabelle whispered, "I'm so terribly sorry, Sam. Smythe's note was misplaced, then the solicitors were held up by a sloppy clerk. Chief-Inspector Hayes was delayed by another case." Tears rolled down her cheeks.

Bleary-eyed, Sam held out his left arm. She took his hand, and he kissed her fingers. "Why are you crying?" He looked into Isabelle's blue eyes, now soft with tears. The drug made his limbs feel heavy and slurred his speech. "You probably saved Elly's life. If she hadn't learned about her family, she would never have had the gumption to push that bastard out the window."

Isabelle squeezed his hand. "The poor child thinks she murdered him."

"If she hadn't done it to him, he might have done it to her. I love happy endings." He relaxed his grip and drifted off to sleep.

Isabelle gently pulled her hand away, wiped her eyes and looked at the doctor. "He's half dead, and calls it a happy ending." She shook her head and glanced under the table. Rex had fallen asleep, a chewing bone in his teeth.

She turned and saw a group of servants huddled in the corner. A large older woman was scowling. Isabelle walked over and spoke softly. "Are you the cook?"

"Yes, My Lady." The elderly woman looked down, then made an awkward curtsy on large feet. "Mrs. Johnson's m' name."

"Well, Mrs. Johnson, if my cook had her kitchen turned into an infirmary at a moment's notice, she'd be very cross indeed... especially when there were such wonderful plans for tomorrow."

The cook nodded sadly. "Won't be haven' n' party now, ma'am. Not wi' t' master…" She shook her head.

"No, Mrs. Johnson. Surely no one expected this evening to end the way it did."

The servants looked bleakly at each other. Some of the women sobbed quietly.

Isabelle sadly smiled at each one, in turn. "Constable Wright is arranging distribution of the wonderful food you've all prepared. It would be a crime to waste it."

"Aye, yer right about that. Thank 'ee, My Lady." She curtsied again and turned to her staff. "Nothin' to do 'ere, then. Off y' go now, double-time." The servants scurried away.

Only Mary the serving maid remained. She had never seen a titled lady and spoke with a tremor in her voice. "P' Pardon, My Lady."

"Yes?"

She starred at Sam. "Will 'e be alright, then?"

"The doctor said his arm should heal. He's not sure about internal injuries."

Mary nodded, then sniffed back tears.

Isabelle was surprised. "Do you know each other?"

"Aye, M' Lady. We met this afternoon."

"Well, he's sleeping now. Do you want to sit with him?"

"Oh, may I, M' Lady? May I, please?"

"Of course."

Mary silently placed a chair next to Sam and sat down.

Wondering how Sam made this girl fall in love with him that fast, Isabelle went upstairs to the drawing room.

Elly's empty soup mug was by her side. Chief-Inspector Hayes sat beside her. His short grey hair and thick moustache were slightly mussed, his eyes were red, and he looked exhausted. His notebook lay opened on a tea-table and he impatiently tapped his pencil on the polished wood.

"Miss Roundtree, please let me be the judge of what is or is not relevant. Please, let's go over this again."

Desperate for sleep, Elly closed her eyes. "I've already told you everything."

The Chief-Inspector spoke softly and distinctly. "Sir John was leaning against the window. The glass was loose and he fell…"

"I pushed him…"

"Miss Roundtree!" He jumped to his feet and saw Isabelle in the doorway. "Thank goodness! Lady Richfield, I need your assistance. Please take my chair." He turned back. Elly's eyes were closed. "Please, Miss Roundtree, you must not sleep. Not just yet. I do not mean to distress you..."

Isabelle hurried over. "You seem to be distressing her a great deal. Chief-Inspector, if you could finish with my ward as soon as possible, I would be very grateful."

At the word "ward," Elly's eyes flew open.

He spoke quietly. "I hope to finish momentarily, M' Lady, but please, sit down. There is something vitally important we must all resolve, right now."

Isabelle trusted the Chief-Inspector. He was a caring and compassionate professional. She sat down and waited.

He pulled over another chair, sat heavily, and rubbed his tired eyes. Collecting his thoughts, he weighed the possible consequences of what he was about to do. Exchanging blind-justice for reasonable-mercy, he turned to Elly. "Miss Roundtree, you have just been through a terrible ordeal. Tonight, in your presence, two men were killed."

Elly tried to sit up, but pain in her shoulder pulled her back. "I didn't see Father Folen... I only heard the shot. Then I ran..."

He held up a hand. "You ran to help you fiancé."

Both women looked confused.

Leaning into them, he spoke very softly and slowly. "The gunshot startled your fiancé, causing him to fall back through the loose window glass." Elly shook her head, and the Chief-Inspector gently touched her arm. "Miss Roundtree. Sir John told you that he was responsible for your father's death."

She nodded.

"He also told you, that he was marrying you *only* for your estate."

She whispered, "He also wanted sons. I told you..." The memory of his threat was so vivid, she wanted to cry.

"And, what do you suppose would have happened to you, even if you had done your duty, and produced his sons?"

"He said..."

"Would you still have been useful to him? Or would you merely have been a constant reminder of his murderous past?"

She hesitated. "I don't know."

The Chief-Inspector rubbed his forehead. "This afternoon, Lady Richfield told me that she feared for your life. I believe her fears were well founded."

Isabelle squeezed Elly's hand. "Thank God, you're safe."

The Chief-Inspector nodded. "Yes, Miss Roundtree. You are safe, because you defended yourself against your potential murderer." Both women looked pale, as he continued. "Although we three know this to be true…" Leaning in even closer, he gave himself a moment, deciding that the brutal truth would be best. "In a court of law," he took a deep breath, "a jury of arrogant men, who believe that women are chattel, might believe that a woman responsible for the death -- of even the worst scoundrel -- should be hanged."

Both women stared at him. Elly blurted out. "He fell back through the loose window glass. I ran to help him and I fell as well. It wasn't my fault." Now terrified, she stared at the Chief-Inspector.

Grateful for an excuse to move, Isabelle fumbled in her sleeve and found a handkerchief. "It's a tragedy. This was to be the poor child's wedding day. Anyone can see that she's heartbroken."

"Yes. It is a terrible loss." The Chief-Inspector sat back, relieved. "By rights, Miss Roundtree should be available for further questioning by the local police constable. Fortunately, the simple soul is so in awe of me, he'll follow my instructions without question. I'll see that he doesn't trouble you, again. Your aunt is the only witness. Fortunately, her hysteria will make her testimony unreliable. Miss Roundtree, what will become of her now?"

Elly sighed sadly. "Auntie will never leave this house. She told me a hundred times that she was born here and wishes to stay here always. She's welcome to it. I never want to see it again."

The Chief-Inspector nodded. "Very well then, we agree that Father Folen was murdered, and Sir John died by misadventure." He shared an exhausted smiled with Isabelle. They both sighed with relief. "Miss Roundtree, you shouldn't be bothered again, at least anytime soon. There will be an inquest, and a judge will eventually try your father - uncle - whatever he is. Assize judges are notoriously slow reaching villages this far from London. Roundtree may rot in jail for months before he is finally tried. He's sure to be speedily hanged, so it hardly matters. Tonight, my sergeant and I will stay at the pub in town. We should clear up all the details in a day or two, then…"

Angry voices sounded from downstairs, and Isabelle rushed to the kitchen. She found Sam sitting up on the kitchen table. His face was grey and his eyes sunken. His bare chest was a ghastly collage of red and purple marks crisscrossing an old scar. The white plaster cast hung like a deformed wing at his side.

Dr. Vickers's hands were on his hips. "You're a damn fool, Smelling. That cast is barely dry. Your ribs are cracked. You could puncture a lung and die. Is it worth risking your life for a bloody newspaper story?"

"Yes, doctor, it certainly is." Sam's eyes watered. "This is a great story." He took a painful breath. "I can serialize it." He took another breath. "It'll make a fortune."

"If you live to enjoy it."

"My life won't be worth much, if I let someone else get it."

"Who else, man? There's no one else who knows about it."

"Isabelle!"

"Yes, darling." She hurried to his side.

Sam closed his eyes against the pain. "You wired Settle from London, didn't you?"

"There were two wires: the first from my secretary, procuring a carriage from the station, and the second from the Chief-Inspector, ordering the local constable to meet us."

Sam spoke in short, painful phrases. "If it went over the wire service -- some spy has it -- If I don't get it to *The Times* before -- tomorrow's -- mid-day edition -- someone else will. I've got to get back to London -- tonight. Garingham won't be needing his car. The driver can take me all the way to Skipton."

Mary curtsied. "I'll fetch the chauffeur." She hurried out.

Sam called after her, "Thanks Mary. Look Isabelle, with my arm -- I can't write."

"Not to worry. Bill employs a woman who works one of those typing machines. She's clever. As soon as we get back, I'll set her to work for you."

"Great!" He smiled.

"But darling, this is too dangerous. You…"

"Doctor, wrap me up anyway you have to. I'm leaving."

Sam stood up and staggered two steps.

Dr. Vickers pushed him back toward the table. "All right, man. Stay still while I bind your ribs. Won't take but a few minutes and it could save your life."

"Sam, I'm going with you." They all turned to see Elly, pale and trembling, at the foot of the stairs.

Isabelle's mouth fell open. "Don't be ridiculous, Elly. You're injured. One lunatic among us is enough. I'm not even sure there's a train this late."

Elly limped over to Sam. He took her hand. "Your friend Robert Dennison, I need to see him as soon as we get back."

"Whatever for?"

"If this story gets anywhere near the coverage I think it will, the part about the portrait could make him famous. It'll also make him infamous." He laughed, then doubled over from the pain. "Parents won't want him near their daughters -- and no school will hire him, But - It could get him a lot of commissions. Do you think he'd risk it?"

She laughed. "He'll love it."

At the sound of ripping cloth, Sam sat back and Elly hopped to a chair. Dr Vickers carefully bound Sam's ribs. When he finished, he tore thinner strips and bound Elly's ankle.

Sam took a breath, pushing against his binding. Tears filled his eyes. He was in terrible pain, but not about to admit it.

Isabelle pleaded, "Sam, darling, certainly we can wait until daylight."

He closed his eyes against the pain. "Don't fight me Isabelle -- just help me -- all right?"

"Of course. I'll do whatever you want." Totally exhausted, Isabelle shrugged. "Elly darling, I've tried talking with your aunt. She's huddled in bed, staring at that family portrait. She keeps saying, 'I need to take care of Papa's house.' She doesn't seem to know what happened tonight."

Elly shrugged, "I told you she will never leave."

The dog woke, staggered out from under the table, yawned, leaned against Sam, and nudged him with a wet nose.

Dr. Vickers smiled. "That's some dog. What are you going to do with him?"

Sam scratched Rex behind the ear. "I can't take him to London. I've no idea where he belongs."

"Is he a good watchdog?"

"The best."

The doctor nodded. "Rex!"

The dog looked at Dr. Vickers.

"How would you like to live in the Dales?"

Rex wagged his tail and looked to Sam for approval.

Sam chuckled, "Sounds like a good arrangement to me. Go on boy!" He pointed to Dr. Vickers.

Rex ambled over to the doctor, sat on his foot, looked up, beat his tail against the floor, and panted bad breath.

Dr. Vickers smiled and scratched his head.

Isabelle begged, "Dr. Vickers, please travel with us. I'll pay well for your services, and I can't let Sam be further injured."

Vickers shrugged. "Sorry madam, but I'm the only doctor in this part of the Dales. I'm needed here, and there's nothing you or I can do, to help a fool bent on suicide."

Isabelle wrung her hands. "But Elly insists on traveling, too. I can't possibly handle two invalids by myself."

Mary hurried to Isabelle. "Please, My Lady, take me wi' thee. I'm a good worker and I'm fond o' Sam."

Isabelle nodded. "Of course. I'm grateful for the help."

It was 10:30. A light freezing rain beat against the kitchen windows. Isabelle tried to stay calm calculating train connections. The daytime trip had taken five hours. Night time connections were not as good. The Skipton station house may not be open. They might end up waiting on a cold platform in the rain. This was madness. Why not wait until morning? She looked at Sam. He glared back with fierce blue eyes, daring her to delay the trip. She said nothing and braced herself for a horrible journey.

Chapter Fourteen

Mary took Sam's jacket and coat, opened the right seams, and removed the right arms. He cautiously slid off the kitchen table and braced himself as she slid the clothes over his left arm. She arranged the right side over his shoulder and under his cast. With a thick needle and heavy thread, she sewed the clothes together, leaving his cast exposed.

Isabelle was surprised. "Well done, Mary."

Sam said, "Yeah Mary. That's great."

Mary looked pleased with herself as she knotted the thread and cut off the needle. She smiled into Sam's deep blue eyes. "I'd do anythin' for thee, Sam."

He sent Isabelle a crooked smile. "You owe me a suit."

Isabelle laughed and nodded. "At the very least."

Dr. Vickers stood back and crossed his arms. "It's raining. How are you going to keep that cast dry?" Mary was ahead of him, already wrapping a waxed cotton raincoat around the delicate plaster. She bundled extra blankets to take on the train.

Elly used one of her uncle's walking sticks as a cane, and gave another to Sam.

Dr. Vickers shook his head, and gave Sam another shot of morphine.

Chief-Inspector Hayes spoke to Sir John's chauffer. "How much petrol do you have?"

"A full tank, sir. I filled up before I left."

"Good. You can drive Lady Richfield's party all the way to the Skipton train station and return immediately. You and the car are both needed for the murder investigation."

The chauffeur looked worried. "I already told the constable everything I know."

"Fine, then you can tell me when you get back." He turned to Isabelle. "I wish I could help you get to London, but I can't leave the crime scene. There will be an inquest, and you may all need to come back."

Isabelle sighed from exhaustion. "How soon will that be?"

"It depends on the coroner."

Dr. Vickers laughed. "Don't worry, I'm the coroner. For the past twenty years, I've signed every death certificate in the area. Poor Father Folen died from Anthony Roundtree's bullet. No one will challenge that." He grimaced and went upstairs to check on Lillian Roundtree.

The Chief-Inspector watched him go. "Unless Roundtree is daft enough to plead innocent, there won't even be a trial."

Isabelle's shuddered. "I understand. Thank you, Chief-Inspector, you've been extraordinary through all this. Once again, I've dragged you away from your family."

"And, once again, it wasn't your fault -- and once again, thank you for actually believing I have a life other than chasing criminals."

"Did I ever thank you for your speech, last night?" She shook her head in disbelief. "Was that really only last night?"

He chuckled, "It was, and you did thank me. I was happy to assist in a cause close to my heart. Any father of daughters should care about other men's daughters." He looked at Mary, wrapping Sam and Elly in raincoats and mufflers. "Good luck with this lot."

Isabelle sighed. "Thanks, I'll need it. I hope the next time we meet will be a happy event."

"This one could have ended much worse."

Isabelle closed her eyes and breathed deeply. "You're right of course. Good bye." She held out her hand.

He took her hand, looked into her lovely face, smiled, and went back to work.

The chauffeur drove the car close to the front door. Isabelle said a silent prayer as Sam eased into the front seat. The women sat in back, with Elly between Mary and Isabelle. The chauffeur climbed in, next to Sam, and started off.

Elly gazed out the window. The house became smaller and smaller, finally disappearing from view. A feeling of relief washed over her. "I'm never going back there, not ever." She snuggled against Isabelle's shoulder, inhaling her comforting perfume. The car hit a bump and Sam moaned. Elly called, "Sam, are you all right?"

He called back, "Don't you worry about me. I'll have the best story of my career. Soon as this morphine does its job I'll be so sleepy you'll have to carry me onto the train."

Isabelle yawned and stretched her neck. "*When* we get a train. We may be at the station for hours." She cuddled Elly. "But you, my sweet child, are finally safe. I hope there's a telephone at the station. Kathy, Jerry, and your Robert must all be worried sick." She chuckled, "I almost forgot about Rory. He's probably the most worried of all."

She looked past Elly to Mary, huddled tearfully against the car door. "Mary, have you traveled far from the Dales?"

Mary sniffed, "No My Lady. I never been even this far from 'ome."

"Did you like working for Mr. Roundtree?"

She hesitated. "Well, no ma'am. My job as serving maid were fine, but t' Master and Sir John…"

Elly almost screamed. "Oh, Mary -- did they…?"

"They both tried, Miss. I was able to run away each time, but didn't know how much longer they'd let me…" She sniffled and wiped her eyes with her skirt.

Isabelle reached her arm and squeezed Mary's shoulder. "Mary dear, you are very kind to help us on this journey. After we get home, that is -- to London, and you've had a good rest, you can decide if you wish to remain, or come back to Settle. If you choose to remain, I'll give you a reference and help you find a position at one of the big houses. If you wish to go home, you'll be paid for your time with us, and given the train fare back."

"Oh, aye, thank thee My Lady. Thank thee kindly." She sat back as the car drove toward the station.

*

Elly woke with a start. The car had stopped. It was pitch dark and horribly cold. She shivered and rubbed her eyes. All around her was blackness. There wasn't a sound. She leaned into Isabelle but the seat was empty. Frantic, she reached forward for Sam. There was only heavy wool upholstery on empty seats.

"Isabelle? Sam? Mary? Chauffer?" She screamed into the dark. "Where are you? What's happened? Has something happened to Sam?" Frantic that Sam was worse and they had taken him to get help, Elly reached blindly for the door. The car lurched, the door flew open, and the silver gleam of Peg's knife flew at her face. Mick laughed through yellow teeth. Elly screamed and fell down a bottomless pit.

There was a screech of brakes and calls of, "Elly! Elly! Wake up!"

The car skidded to a halt, throwing everyone forward. Isabelle shook Elly. "You're dreaming. Elly! Wake up. It's just a bad dream."

Elly was drenched with sweat, her heart pounding out of her chest. She clutched Isabelle. "I'm sorry. I'm so sorry." Sam, Mary, and the chauffeur stared at her.

Isabelle held her tight. "What was it? Tell me what you were dreaming?"
Elly shook her head and sat back sobbing.

Her scream had panicked everyone. It was a few minutes before the chauffeur was calm enough to continue driving.

Afraid of dreaming again, Elly clenched her teeth to stay awake. She silently recited every song and poem she had ever learned.

Skipton Station was dark and deserted. Isabelle cursed silently. She wanted everyone to wait in the warm car, but the poor chauffeur was a mess of nerves. "I'm sorry, M' Lady, but t' Chief-Inspector told me to return immediately. I've got t' go back."

Isabelle clenched her jaw and tossed a waxed cotton rain slicker over her coat. She bundled her wounded troops out of the car and onto the windy platform. The car drove away, leaving them alone. The rain had stopped and slight moonlight illuminated the station awning. Like refugees, Elly and Sam huddled together on a narrow bench. Mary wrapped the extra blankets around them, then sat as close to Sam as his cast allowed. Soon, all three were asleep. Isabelle paced the dark windy platform, cursing, willing a train to magically appear. As the minutes crawled by she became more and more angry.

Sam moaned in his sleep. She spun around, whispering through gritted teeth, "Serves you right. Obstinate fool! All this pain for a stupid story."

She caught her breath. He was pale and shivering. She protectively adjusted the blankets around all three. Mary woke, saw her mistress, and started to stand. Isabelle put a finger to her lips and motioned for the girl to stay where she was. There were beads of sweat on Sam's face. Isabelle felt his cheeks and forehead.

"He's got a fever. I'll brew him some Maidenhair tea when we get home. There's nothing I can do for him now." Shivering, she snuggled down next to Elly. The girl's screaming nightmare still rang in her ears. She whispered, "What really happened to you? I'm sure you haven't told us half of it."

*

Elly woke up warm under blankets, cuddled between Sam and Isabelle. The rain had stopped. Across the tracks, a lighted SKIPTON station sign shone clear in the fresh fragrant air. A dark mist blew off the side of the sign. It was pretty. She had never seen mist that colour. She yawned, wondering if there was a lake on the other side. What was making it glow like that? There was no moon. It was too early for the sun. Through heavy

98

eyelids she could see the mist became thicker, longer. Funny, it looked like horsehair. Almost asleep, she giggled. "It's not horsehair, silly. It's a girl's hair. It's so pretty, long and dark. It's Peg's hair." The hair burst into flame. Witch eyes like hot coals flew at her.

"Come on Princess, daddy's waitin'!"

"NO! NO!"

"Elly! Oh, my, Elly! You're having another dream, wake up."

This time Elly thought her heart would explode from her chest. She threw off the blankets and ran down the platform, eyes bulging, and sweat running down her face. Her ankle throbbed, but she barely noticed the pain. Mary covered Sam with blankets as Isabelle chased Elly down the dark walkway.

She caught the girl, threw her arms around her, and held her still. "Elly, what did you dream? Tell me."

"Peg!" Elly's eyes were wild, her voice strained. "There! Behind the sign." She stopped and stared. "Where's the sign? There was a sign."

"The dream in the car, what did you see?"

"That was Mick, with Peg's knife." Her legs collapsed and she sunk onto the moist wooden planks.

Isabelle went down with her. "Tell me about the knife. What really happened? I know there's more than you told the Chief-Inspector."

Elly shook her head and lay in a dejected heap.

Isabelle sat back, clutching her own pounding heart. "And I was worried about Sam." After a few minutes, Elly quieted and slowly rolled into a ball. Her ankle throbbed.

Isabelle spoke in a monotone. "I'll kill Sam for this trip… Once he's well enough." Elly chuckled and Isabelle lay down next to her on the hard, wet wood. They looked sideways at each other and started to giggle. The absurd situation, and overwhelming fatigue, set them both into fits of laughter.

Elly's throat tightened. "I'm so frightened."

Isabelle sighed and closed her eyes, "It's over, darling. There's nothing more to be frightened of."

"They're still out there… Mick and Peg. I think Tommy Quinn's left the country."

"They have no reason to harm you, now. I'd be very surprised if Peg was still in England. From what you've said, Mick hasn't the wit to act alone. It's the middle of the night after the worst day of your life. Nothing looks good now. Give it a few days. Everything will look much brighter, I promise."

*

The train arrived at 11:33 p.m., and four bedraggled gypsies gratefully boarded a first class carriage. At 11:45 the train pulled out and Isabelle sent Mary to the dining car. She managed to rouse the sleeping chef, and all four devoured a very good supper. Isabelle was pleased that Sam and Elly had appetites.

Elly stayed close to Isabelle. Sitting across from them, Mary kept Sam propped up with blankets. The pained look on his face had softened. The ride was smooth, the sound of the wheels hypnotic, and all four fell asleep. As Elly's eyelids began to close, she glanced out the window into the black night. Sir John Garingham's face flashed in the glass and she jumped forward, her heart racing. She almost screamed, but stopped herself. Another nightmare might mean she was mad. They would send her to Bedlam. Isabelle, Sam, and Mary all slept soundly. Relieved, Elly smiled to herself and sat up straight. She tried to stay awake for the rest of the trip.

Chapter Fifteen

London, January 6, 1904

They arrived in London shortly before 5:00 a.m. and caught a hansom to 140 Piccadilly on the corner of Hamilton Place. Isabelle had never been so glad to be home.

Mary was dead on her feet. Isabelle turned her over to the housekeeper with orders she be treated kindly and given a bed in the servants' quarters.

Elly was put to bed and Isabelle brewed her Wild Opium Lettuce tea. The girl was soon in a deathlike sleep.

Isabelle forced Sam to drink a strong tea of four parts Maidenhair to three parts Shrub Strawberry. His fever broke within the hour. At 5:30 Miss Blackwell, Lord Richfield's typewriter, took Sam's dictation.

At 6:30 a.m. Lord Richfield's footman rushed a copy to the *London Times*. Another copy was telegraphed to the *New York Times*.

Despite his physical pain, Sam was ecstatic. He was finally put to bed in a room next to Elly. Isabelle brewed him Wild Opium Lettuce tea. He was still in pain and dozed fitfully.

With both patients tucked away, Isabelle finally began to relax.

At 7:30 a.m. Lord Richfield's physician, Dr. Cummings, examined the two patients. He spoke to Isabelle while closing his medical case. "That country doctor's skill is impressive. Couldn't have fashioned a better plaster myself. Did it on a kitchen table, you say?" She smiled and he nodded with approval. "I'll leave those rib bindings in place, for now. The girl should do well after a good rest. I'm prescribing laudanum…"

Isabelle shook her head. "Thank you doctor, but you know I prefer my own remedies." Dr. Cummings sighed and tried to sound stern. "Very well, Lady Richfield. I gave up arguing with you about medicines long ago. In all other areas you are a most reasonable woman. Of course, your family complains of fewer ailments than most, so…" he raised his hands and shrugged. "I shall look in on your patients this evening. In the meantime, you need rest as much they do." He waved a warning finger. "'Physician, heal thy self.'" He bowed, started to go, and turned back. "Oh, by the way, well done on the school for girls. We need more reformers, like you." He smiled and left the house.

At 8:30 a.m., Isabelle called Gildstein Gallery and told Robert Dennison what had happened. He was frantic to see Elly, but waiting for prospective clients to view his paintings. Isabelle assured him, "There's no rush, Mr. Dennison. I've given Elly a strong opiate. She'll sleep for hours. Please secure your commissions. That's what she'd want. Anytime you wish to come here, day or night, you're very welcome."

Relieved, but totally exhausted, Isabelle wandered between Sam and Elly. She taught servants how to apply cooling liniments of Lobelia, Black Cohosh, Calendula, and alcohol to both patients' bruises. Dr. Vickers was right, and Elly's pain was worsening. The purple bruise on her forehead had spread down her cheek and was turning chartreuse. Her ankle was pale-violet and horribly swollen. Her shoulder was an alarming deep-purple.

As the opiate wore off, Elly's sleep lightened and she began dreaming. Isabelle was with Sam when she heard Elly scream. She sped next door and found the girl tossing fitfully. It was too soon after the last treatment, but Isabelle brewed Elly another cup of tea. If the child didn't sleep, no healing could begin.

Shortly after 10:00 a.m., Isabelle called His Majesty's Theatre. The secretary answered the telephone and went to fetch Katherine Stewart. He found her in the rehearsal hall, sitting behind the director's table, smiling as she watched Jeremy O'Connell stage THE TEMPEST.

Jeremy stood in the middle of the large empty space. He was taller than the other men, and held his long body taught. His dark eyes were focused on a faraway vision. He spoke in a whisper meant only for the ten actors immediately near him. They appeared to be mesmerized, concentrating to hear his every word. Jeremy stood perfectly still, staring into the distance. He raised one finger to his lips. Following the focus of his eyes, the finger gracefully lifted. His arm followed, pointing to the top of an imaginary hill. The movement seemed to pull his lithe body, willing it to take flight. The secretary was entranced. As wonderful as Jeremy O'Connell was on stage, he was magical, creating new worlds.

The secretary tiptoed to Katherine and whispered that Lady Richfield was on the telephone. Katherine sprung up and hurried to the office.

*

After Isabelle told her the story, Katherine hung up the phone and took a few moments to gather her thoughts. It was horrifying. Elly could have been killed. Sam Smelling very nearly was killed. She shook her head.

All's Well That Ends Well. Thank God they were both safe. She hurried back to the rehearsal hall eager to tell the news. Jeremy was still in a dreamlike state. Very gently, she tapped him on the shoulder, then jumped back, before he could curse the interruption.

She said, "Isabelle has Elly." He stopped cold. The entire room of actors and crew rushed to hear the news. She retold the story. By the end she was trembling.

Before Jeremy could speak, Rory was at his arm. "Jerry, I've got to see Elly, please let me go... Please!"

"No." Jeremy moved away.

"Please?" Beads of sweat popped out on the young man's brow. He blocked Jeremy's way. "I'm going, Jerry. With or without your permission. I'd rather it was with."

Jeremy's mouth fell open. His back arched and his eyes blazed. "Who the bloody hell do you think you are? No one leaves my rehearsal." In the past, Rory had pleaded for favours, even begged and cried. This time he gave his master an ultimatum. Jeremy's loss of control felt alarming. "How dare you?"

"Please, Jerry. I won't be gone long. Please?" Rory's throat tightened. His sudden flash of courage evaporated. He looked up into Jeremy's fierce dark eyes. "Please?"

Rory was behaving like a boy again and Jeremy was relieved. "All right, be back in an hour." He walked away.

Rory gasped, "An hour? I can't get there and back..."

"ONE HOUR!"

"Yes, sir. Thanks!"

*

Rory grabbed his coat and ran full speed out the door. He did not stop running until he found a hansom. The ride was short, and he was still breathless when he rang the bell at Hamilton Place.

Smythe answered the door. "Good morning, Mr. Cook. Miss Fielding's in her usual room and Mr. Smelling is down the hall. Her Ladyship..."

"Thank you, Smythe." Rory was already halfway up the stairs. Elly's door was ajar and he pushed it open. The curtains were closed and it took his eyes a moment to adjust to the dim light.

A maid sat near the dark window. She curtsied, and whispered, "'Mornin' Mr. Cook. Shall I tell Her Ladyship you're here?"

"Yes, please."

She left the room, leaving the door open.

Rory tossed his coat over a chair and walked to the bed. Elly was asleep, her hair strewn wildly across the pillow. Her skin was chalk white and an ugly bruise spread from her forehead down her cheek. His throat tightened and he swallowed hard.

"Too much of water hast thou, poor Ophelia,
And therefore I forbid my tears…"

A teacup sat on the bedside table. There were only a few drops of liquid in the bottom, but he recognized the aroma. "Poor Elly. If you drank this, you won't even know I've been here."

He sat on the edge of the bed. Elly did not stir. Her breathing was shallow. He stroked her cheek. She stayed still. He leaned over and gently kissed her lips. She moved very slightly, so he did it again. The third time, she opened her eyes. Her face broke into a sweet smile and she tried to put her arms around his neck. Her right shoulder was so sore she moaned and let her arm drop.

"Rory…" Her voice was a slurred whisper. "I'm so glad you've come."

"I can only stay a few minutes. I have to get back to rehearsal."

She forced her eyes open.

"Go back to sleep, darling. Don't try to stay awake."

She closed her eyes and was instantly asleep.

He heard the swish of a skirt as Isabelle shuffled toward the bed. She rubbed her eyes and dragged her feet. Rory sat up and wrapped his arms around her waist. She hugged his shoulder and kissed the top of his head. He pulled her down beside him and she collapsed like a rag doll. The bed swayed, but Elly did not stir.

He whispered, "You've given her Wild Opium Lettuce tea."

She raised an eyebrow.

"And you've covered her with a liniment of Lobelia, Black Cohosh, and alcohol."

"You forgot the Calendula."

"No, I didn't know about that one. That's an extra. I always loved the smell of that liniment. It's powerful. I had a nanny who preferred the old ways, like you, Priestess."

She laughed wearily. "My, but you flatter me."

104

They were silent for a few minutes. He watched Elly sleep. "She looks awful. So do you."

"Thank you." Isabelle stood up, walked away, and collapsed into an easy chair.

"I've got to get back to rehearsal. Jerry only gave me an hour."

"I'm surprised he gave you that."

"I had to grovel for it."

She laughed and her head fell back.

Rory looked at Elly. "She's all right, isn't she?"

Isabelle closed her eyes. "Two doctors say she'll be fine. I'm worried about her mind."

He spun around. "Why?"

"She refuses to talk about what happened, except the broadest details. Since she won't talk, she's having terrible nightmares."

"But it's too soon to tell." He was short of breath. "You can't know... Surely, after she's had a good sleep, some healing, some time..."

"I hope so."

"She's sleeping peacefully now."

"I've given her enough opium tea to dope an elephant."

His vision blurred and he wiped his eyes with the palm of his hand. "She's got to be all right; after all she's gone through... How's Sam?"

"Physically a wreck, but so ecstatic about his story he'll probably be up and about before she will."

Rory looked at the clock. "I wish I could stay. Can I come back?"

"Of course you can. Don't be stupid."

He laughed. "My but you're cranky when you're tired. Why don't you go to bed? You'll be ill yourself. They'll be all right now. The servants can look after them."

"I will, soon. You'd better go."

He looked back at Elly. "It's the Scottish Play tonight. I won't be able to come back before tomorrow."

"I don't expect any changes before then."

Common sense screamed he should go, but he felt glued to Elly's bedside. He swallowed back a lump in his throat. "The day Elly arrived was like a dream. When she walked on stage for her audition, I thought the world had spun in a different direction. She was so beautiful. She opened her mouth and it spun back a bit." He laughed. "She was terrible. Jerry saw something I didn't. He thinks he can teach her to act. I don't care what she does." Tears filled his eyes. He whispered, "Damn it! Why can't she love me?"

Half asleep, Isabelle sighed, "She does. Oh my, men are so daft. She adores you."

"She's afraid of me."

"Yes... and for good reason."

"Why, what's there to be afraid of?"

Isabelle started laughing and continued for longer than Rory liked.

"What the bloody hell's so funny?"

"Come here." She opened her arms.

He knelt beside her and laid his head in her lap. "Isabelle, that night -- your Christmas Eve ball, you looked like the most fantastically beautiful witch."

"Did I really?" She chuckled. "Well, you looked absolutely adorable, in white tie and tails. Your golden hair was shiny-clean and smartly cut." She ran her fingers through his now overlong, messy hair. "I wanted to eat you with a spoon. Actually, I wanted -- you -- badly. I didn't think I'd ever get you. Later, when we met in the hall, you were so angry. By then I was determined to have you, but the only way was to make you angrier still. You made me pay for my... witchcraft."

He looked up. "What do you mean, I made you pay?" The colour drained from his face. "Did I hurt you?"

"You came close."

He whispered, "I pulled out, didn't I?"

"You did. You were very considerate," she chuckled.

"I'm sorry. I..."

"I invited it, don't reproach yourself. I knew exactly what I was doing." She ran a finger down his cheek and smiled seductively. "And... You more than made up for it later... but... my virile angel, Elly hasn't invited it. She's a child, a wounded one at that. With all my experience, I could barely handle you. She's very smart to be afraid of you."

"She's going back to that bastard who raped her."

"No!" She clutched his shoulder. "It wasn't rape. We don't know this man, and we don't know who she is when she's with him. Whatever they had together, it will never be what it was, and he's a terribly important part of her life. If you really love her, you'll be there to help her through whatever comes of it."

"Even if it means letting her go?"

"Even then."

Tears sprung into his eyes. "What if I lose her?"

"Then she was never yours to begin with." Her eyes were closing.

He sighed, stood up, and very lightly kissed her lips. "Get some sleep." He grabbed his coat and flew out the door.

Chapter Sixteen

It was noon when Sir William Richfield arrived home from his trip. When Smythe explained the events of the past thirty hours, he bellowed, "Why the bloody hell wasn't I notified?"

Smythe trembled. "Forgive me sir, but everything happened so quickly, Lady Richfield handled all the details herself. Mr. Smelling telephoned the night before and said that Miss Fielding was in danger. I left the note where Her Ladyship was sure to see it, but..."

A harried nanny raced down the stairs. "Please, Sir William, it's my fault. Please don't blame Mr. Smythe. The children painted pictures for Her Ladyship. I didn't see the note and let the children cover it up. Her Ladyship didn't see the note until the next day, forgive me..." Hysterically weeping, she fell at Sir William's feet.

Sir William stomped past her, up the stairs, "Yes, yes, you're both forgiven. Now, where's my wife? Pig-headed woman!"

He found Isabelle asleep in the chair in Elly's room. He gently touched her shoulder. She opened her eyes and smiled.

"Good God, Isabelle! What's happened to you?"

She looked ten years older than when he had left. Her startling blue eyes were tiny, red, sore, and sunken into deep black circles. Her complexion was chalky and her skin was taut. Even her hair seemed to have lost its sheen. She stood up, gratefully reaching her arms around his neck. His comforting arms closed protectively around her, as he kissed her eager mouth. A few feet away, Elly slept soundly. He looked with horror at Elly's bruised face. Isabelle took him next door where Sam Smelling lay, beaten and battered. He was finally sound asleep.

Sir William took Isabelle's hand. "You're coming to my room so I can keep my eye on you." He rang for Charleston, and ordered her to put her mistress to bed.

While the women were busy, he summoned Smythe and the housekeeper. "No one is to disturb Her Ladyship. No one. Do you understand?"

Smythe answered for both. "We do, Sir William. Lady Richfield's already trained some of the servants to nurse the invalids."

"Good. Now bring us some food, and leave us alone. I want someone stationed outside this door so no one gets in or out."

Isabelle was served lunch on a bed tray, and Sir William on a small table by her side. He dismissed the servants, looked at the two meals and laughed. "I can't remember the last time we had a picnic." Isabelle toyed with her food, then began eating and devoured everything. She finished quickly and started telling him the story. Listening silently, his appetite shrunk with each horrid detail.

Comforted by the food and the soft bed, Isabelle sank back and closed her eyes. "Elly was so looking forward to her first rehearsal and her young man coming to town."

"He arrived, I assume."

"Yes," she yawned. "He's coming over this evening."

"What's he like? I should be concerned, shouldn't I, now that the girl's our responsibility?"

Isabelle laughed. "I've only spoken to him on the telephone, but he sounds charming." She held out her hand. "Come here, darling."

He moved her bed tray to the floor, slipped off his boots and jacket and cuddled next to her.

"Elly's going to be our ward, but she's not our child. It's going to be a tricky balance, finding her a place between society and the theatre, but that's my job. Save your fatherly concerns for Lucy." She kissed him. "She'll be giving us grey hairs soon enough." He laughed and kissed her deeply. She clung to him. "Bill darling, I love you so much. Have you any idea what a remarkable husband you are?"

"I don't know. Some of my friends think I'm a damn fool, letting my wife do whatever she pleases."

She caught her breath. "Do they really? You never mentioned it."

He smiled and shrugged. "Why should I bother you with foolish gossip?"

"What sort of gossip?" She sat up, her brows pulled together.

"It's nothing at all. Just gossip from bored men who have nothing better to do than sit in stuffy clubs, prattling like old women." He hugged her tightly. "I think my wife is the most remarkable woman in London. Whatever pleases her is fine with me." He shook his head. "As long as *this* sort of adventure is only once in a lifetime."

"Oh, pray God, yes."

"Looking at Elly, just now -- she looked so young."

"She is young."

109

"You weren't much older when I married you."

"A few months older. Lucy came soon after."

"Your mother was against us."

"She thought I was too young."

"You were too young, but I couldn't wait. I knew you loved me, but I was terrified that you'd wake up one day, take a good look at me, change your mind, and go off with a more dashing chap. There were enough of them sniffing around you."

"I didn't care for any of them."

"Well, I couldn't be sure. That's why I pushed you. I was so afraid of losing you." He was silent for a moment. "Then, after we were married," he sighed. "Was it awful? Did you hate me?"

"Bill, don't." She smiled fondly. "We had growing pains, that was all. We grew up very well, together. We have three redheaded terrors in the nursery to prove it."

He laughed. "Yes we do. And now, my lovely witch," he stood up and walked towards his dresser. "I shall brew you a cup of your Wild Opium Lettuce tea so you can sleep as soundly as your patients."

"Thanks, darling, but I don't need it."

"It won't hurt."

"No, really, I don't want any."

"I don't want you getting up, checking on them every hour. I can do that."

She laughed, "I'll sleep fine without it, I promise."

"I'm serious, I want you out cold. You're overtired."

"And I'm serious that I don't want it."

"It's doing well for Sam and Elly."

"They're injured, I'm not."

"I know you." He took out a large snuffbox and a tea mug. "This is the only way to insure that you sleep."

"No, darling, thank you."

"This brew is wonderful. You've even given light doses to the children."

"Not before they were born."

He stopped dead. "What did you say?"

She put her hands over her eyes, waiting for his moment of wrath, which would fizzle as soon as it had begun.

He spun around and glared at her. "You went off, on a wild chase across the country, knowing that you're expecting a child?"

She nodded, keeping her head down.

He bellowed, "Of all the damn, stupid, pig-headed things you've ever done," he threw the tea mug across the room, smashing it against the wall.

She kept her head down. There was no sound. She slowly raised her eyes.

He glared at her, feet spread apart, hands on hips.

She spoke softly. "I wasn't sure until just now."

He stayed still.

"It'll be September, I think."

His features softened. "Was it Christmas night?"

She smiled, "I think so."

He looked down and laughed. She lay back into the soft pillows.

He asked, "You're all right?"

"I'm fine. Just tired. The child is fine." She laughed. "Just tired."

Smiling, he pulled the covers around her, kissed her, put on his boots and jacket, pulled the curtains closed and walked from the room. He stopped at the door, turned back, and looked at his wife. "My God, you're marvellous. Don't know what I did to deserve you." He glanced towards heaven. "Thanks!" He left the room.

Chapter Seventeen

Robert Dennison was bursting with excitement. Three commissions all but assured his remaining in London.

It was near 7:00 p.m. when he arrived at 140 Piccadilly. The cabby assured him that it was the correct house. It was four stories of ornately carved white stone, and took up the entire corner of Hamilton Place. He stood outside, peering into the windows, and could see crystal chandeliers, parquet floors, huge mirrors, gold wall ornaments, and velvet curtains.

He took a deep breath, walked up to the magnificent mahogany door, raised the glistening brass bell pull, and laughed to himself. "If it's the wrong house, I'll pretend I'm a tradesman."

A maid answered the door. "Good evening, sir."

"Good evening, I'm Robert Dennison."

"Oh, yes, Mr. Dennison, Miss Fielding is expecting you."

His jaw dropped.

The maid took his coat and hat and asked a footman to show him upstairs. Robert's heart pounded as he followed the servant over polished marble floors, past beautiful wall friezes and very good paintings. Up the grand staircase and down a plush hall, the footman stopped at an open door. He knocked. "Miss Fielding, Mr. Dennison to see you."

"Robert!" Elly sat up in bed, reading. She was wrapped in a blue satin dressing gown. Her hair was tied with a matching satin bow and she looked like a child. She quickly put her book on the bedside table and held out her arms. The right side of her face was badly bruised but her eyes were bright, and her smile inviting.

He lunged at the bed. "Oh, my darling girl." Careful not to squeeze her too tightly, he held her arms and covered the undamaged side of her face with soft kisses. She giggled with pleasure. He kissed her lips very gently and sighed with relief. "I was so worried about you."

"I'm fine." Her smile was radiant.

"I'm sure you are." He sat on the edge of the bed. "Except for that," he looked at the bruise on her forehead, "and your ankle," he grimaced, "and your shoulder. Oh dear."

"They're healing fast."

"Lady Richfield told me you have terrible nightmares."

"All gone." Her smile was forced.

"Really?"

"I've been asleep all day and I didn't have even one."

"She told me she'd drugged you, so you couldn't have any."

"Well it worked." She clenched her jaw.

"Were they very frightening?"

She lowered her eyes. "Yes. They were horrible."

"What were they about?"

Her cheeks flushed. "I thought you wanted to make me feel better?"

"I'm sorry, darling. I'm concerned, that's all."

"I know you are." She patted the bed.

He sat next to her and took a deep breath. "I have some very good news."

"Tell me."

"In less than forty-eight hours, I'll know if I'm staying in London."

She sat up, excited. "What happened?"

"Well, three clients have commissioned portraits, all because of *Autumn Lady*. Mr. Gildstein insists they pay a deposit within forty-eight hours, so we'll know just before the school term starts. Once school is in session, I'll be locked in until spring. The commissions will have to go to another artist, and…" He shook his head and put his hands together. "Just pray that by noon on Saturday…"

"Oh, please God! This is so exciting."

A woman's mellow voice asked, "Are we invoking a deity this evening?"

"Isabelle." Elly giggled and held out her hand.

Robert leapt off the bed, nearly tripping over his feet.

Isabelle laughed, "You looked so comfortable, I'm sorry to disturb you."

Robert's eyes bulged at a vision in the doorway.

Sheathed in a white silk kimono, Isabelle leaned comfortably against the door. Her thick chestnut hair was brushed loose over her shoulders. "Please forgive my appearance but, like your young lady, I have been asleep all afternoon. Feeling as tired as I still do, I shall probably be asleep again in a couple of hours. I'm Isabelle Richfield." She offered her hand.

"Of course you are. I'm Robert Dennison." He kissed her hand and held it. "Lady Richfield, how can I ever thank you, for all you've done for Elly?"

"You just did," she smiled. "Do sit down." Perching on the edge of the bed, she took a moment to study Robert Dennison. He was tall, slim, and absolutely stunning. She turned back to Elly. "You look better."

113

Elly smiled. "I feel much better. Dr. Cummings was surprised."

"He's been here already?" Isabelle took Elly's book from the bedside table. It was a beautifully bound volume of Elizabeth Barrett Browning's *Sonnets From The Portuguese.*

Elly nodded. "The doctor said the oddest thing."

"Oh, what was that?" Isabelle read a hand-written note in the front of the book.

"He said, 'I don't approve of Lady Richfield's administrations, but they do seem effective.'" Isabelle raised an eyebrow, so Elly continued. "Why doesn't he approve of them?"

"He is a man, darling. That is all. Most men are vain and arrogant." She looked at Robert. "Present company excluded, of course." He laughed without the slightest embarrassment, and Isabelle was pleased. "Most men believe that the stupidest among them is more capable that the most brilliant of women." She looked back at Robert. "Am I wrong, Mr. Dennison?"

"No, Lady Richfield." He smiled and shook his head. "I am ashamed to say that you understand my sex very well."

Liking him even more, Isabelle smiled and thumbed through the book. "It was sweet of Simon Camden to send this poetry book. It's terribly romantic stuff."

Elly bit her lip. "It's a get well gift. I suppose Miss Stewart told him I'd been injured."

Isabelle raised an eyebrow. "I didn't know you and he were so well acquainted." Elly looked shocked and Isabelle wanted to laugh out loud. Instead, she changed the subject. "So, why were you two invoking the gods?"

Elly clapped her hands. "Robert has three commissions. If they pay their deposits by Saturday, he can stay in London."

"Oh, I am pleased. Congratulations!"

He held up his hands. "It's a bit early for that."

"I wonder who your clients are. If I know them, I could... No, better I don't interfere."

Elly lay back and bit her lip. "This makes it all worthwhile."

Robert's smile vanished. "Makes what, all worthwhile?"

"All the fear. All the pain." The girl was deep in thought.

Robert and Isabelle exchanged worried glances.

Elly sat up. "I was afraid someone would see *Autumn Lady* and find me. They did find me, but if the painting hadn't been shown, you might not have won those commissions." She smiled joyously. "You'll be a success and I'll soon be well, so it was all worth it."

Robert looked serious. "What about Sam Smelling? Does he think it was worth it?"

"Of course! He'll serialize his story."

Isabelle asked quietly, "How can he do that, if you won't tell him about your abduction?"

Elly froze. She looked at Isabelle, then at Robert, then back again. Both faces were like stone. She fell back into the pillows. No one spoke. Slowly, tears filled her eyes. "Telling the story will be like living it all over again. I'm not sure I can."

Isabelle held her hand. "Not telling it is like swallowing a bomb. It's already exploding into nightmares."

"I may not have any more nightmares."

"Maybe not. But what about Sam? Don't you owe him something?"

"I owe him everything. He saved my life."

"Well then?" Isabelle raised a questioning eyebrow and waited.

Elly looked to Robert. He looked back, concerned. She bit her lip. "Is Sam all right? Can I see him?"

Isabelle stood and stretched. "I'll go see if he's awake." She smiled a goodbye, and glided down the hall. Sam's door was open, so she walked in.

"Isabelle! Finally! Come in, I want to show you something."

She was horrified to see her beautiful guest room a mess of filthy newspapers. They were scattered over the bed and piled on the floor.

Sam awkwardly held a huge page with his one good hand. "I've never seen you with your hair down. You look like an angel."

"Thank you." She took the paper from his hand. "You look very well. You've had a wash."

"And a shave. I love having servants."

She laughed. "They even washed your hair." She pushed the soft brown mass back off his forehead. "You need to cut it."

"Never! It's the only way I get beautiful women to pay attention to me."

She sent him a crooked smile, sat on the edge of the bed, and read down the page. "You made the midday edition, then?"

"Yeah." He stared at her.

"Good. If we'd suffered that hideous journey, and you hadn't made it, I would have killed you."

He laughed and looked ashamed. "I'm sorry, but it was worth it."

"I hope so." She read further. "What did Dr. Cummings say?"

"He's surprised how quickly I'm healing."

"Good."

"He wants to cut off the rib bindings tomorrow."

"So soon?" She looked at him. "You must be healing fast."

"I don't know. He poked around my chest and it hurt, a lot."

"Would you rather he left them on?"

"I don't know. I just don't know how much more pain I can take."

"Are you in pain now?"

"Only when I breathe."

"Why didn't you say so? I'll get you something." She stood up.

"Like Opium Lettuce tea? That stuff's powerful. It's amazing I woke up without a headache."

"It never leaves aftereffects. That's why I prefer it to laudanum, the doctor's choice. I'll brew you some Nettle Tree and Hounds Tooth for the pain."

He grimaced. "Sounds delicious."

She laughed. "It's very pleasant actually." She started to leave, and he held out his hand.

"Don't go. I'll drink any bizarre brew you give me, I promise, but don't go yet. You just got here."

She smiled, walked back, and sat down.

"Read the story."

She picked up the paper, found the story, and read silently. He reached with his good hand and ran his fingers through her hair. As she read, her eyes grew large. At the end, she gasped and lowered the page onto her lap. "John Garingham really did engineer Charles Roundtree's murder?"

"That came from the mouth of a dying man."

"So Charles Roundtree's daughter unwittingly avenged her father's death." She took a deep breath. "That's the stuff of Greek tragedy. Does Elly know all this?"

"I don't know how much she knows."

"My God. I wonder how she'll take it."

"It may help. She still feels guilty about pushing that bastard out the window. I think she deserves a medal."

"Just remember -- officially, it was an accident. The man fell. She ran to his aid and was pulled out after him, 'Death by Misadventure'."

"Right." Sam's hair fell over his eyes. She pushed it back and kept her hand on his cheek. He gazed up, adoringly.

"It's a marvellous story, Sam." She sat back. "I'm sure your readers will line up to buy the next episode. What will that be about?"

"Elly's, or rather Elisa's growing up in the Dales, and going off to school. If Dennison will let me, I'll write about his painting *Autumn Lady*."

"Robert Dennison's with her now. It looks like he'll be staying in London, so he should welcome the publicity."

"Dennison's here, now? Great!"

"Are you hungry?"

"Starving."

"Good, so am I. I doubt those two have eaten. I'll ask them to come here, and I'll have some food brought." She stood up and he pulled her back by the hair.

"Ouch! That hurts." She sat down.

"Sorry." He put her hair against his face, inhaled its perfume, and sighed. "I think I hate Bill Richfield."

"For heaven sake, why?"

"He gets to do this every day."

She chuckled. "For thirteen years."

"If you were married to me, I'd never let you out of my sight."

"My, then I'm certainly glad I'm not married to you."

"I'd kill every guy who looked at you the way I'm looking at you, right now."

"The bodies would be piled very high."

He leaned forward, reaching for her face. She easily evaded his kiss. He groaned and lay back. "I hate having only one good arm."

"If you had two, I wouldn't have gotten so close to you."

"Why not? You've got a gaggle of lovers. Why not one more?"

"A gaggle?" She glared at him. "You're got a lot of cheek. What a thing to say."

"Are you flattered or insulted?"

"Honestly, Sam." Her back arched and she crossed her arms. The hint of a smile tickled her lips.

He dropped the end of her hair and lay back. His face contorted in pain.

"Oh dear, let me get you that tea."

"Wait." Exhausted, he closed his eyes. "You know I've been in love with you since the first moment I saw you."

"I doubt that. We met at a party, in New York."

"We saw each other before that, at the racetrack."

"Ah, yes. Bill brought two lovely horses all the way to America. I thought he'd lost his mind."

"They were good horses. He knew what he was doing. They did all right. I was working undercover, investigating a crime syndicate." He touched his chest. "I still have a scar from that knife wound."

She gasped. "So that's the scar on your chest."

"Yeah, it was kind o' like last night. I was bleeding like a pig. At the hospital I refused to lie down and it made the doctor crazy. Then, when I was fresh out of the hospital, a society matron was giving a gala birthday party for a foreign friend. My story made me the hottest new thing in town so I was invited. I didn't want to go, but my girl Rebecca made me."

"We got to the party, and you were the guest of honour. You were wondrous."

Isabelle chuckled, stretched and yawned. "I turned thirty that night. Soon, I'll be thirty-three." She felt his cheek. "You're flushed but there's no fever." I'll get you that tea, and some food."

He stared lovingly as she glided out the door.

*

Elly and Sam passed the next two days sleeping, reading, eating, and talking. They gained strength and felt restless. Sam appreciated Lord Richfield's luxurious hospitality, but missed the privacy of his rented rooms. He had the material for his serialized story, Episode II: the painting of *Autumn Lady* and Episode III: Elly's first month in London. She was finally ready to tell him Episode IV: the abduction.

Elly was still bruised and sore. Just turning from side-to-side was painful. Her dreams were often frightening, but she no longer screamed in her sleep. She was frantic to get back to rehearsals before they replaced her with another pretty girl. Constantly rereading *THE TEMPEST*, she memorized everyone's part.

Rory visited as often as he could, and kept her up-to-date on rehearsals. "It's amazing. Jerry used to give us a sketchy description of what he wanted, then scream when we got it wrong. Now, instead of torturing us, making us play it over-and-over, he glares at Miss Stewart, yells, 'Katie, fix it!' and moves to the next scene.

"She takes his notes, and between rehearsals, carefully explains what he wants. When he watches the scene again, we do it right. He stares and says nothing." Rory shook his head in disgust. "His way of complimenting Miss Stewart is to say nothing. You know he's the only one who calls her Katie. She's Kathy to her other friends. At first we were afraid to even say, 'Katie.' Now, we all yell, 'Katie, fix it!' every time something goes wrong. It's become a mantra."

*

After the Sunday matinee, Jeremy stayed at the theatre for a meeting about smoke effects with Jamie Jamison. Pyrotechnics were needed for lightning during the storm, and island mists.

The Richfield family invited Katherine, Evan, Rory, Robert Dennison, Sam, and Elly for tea. Katherine studied the pale green bruises on Elly's face. "Don't worry darling, you'll soon be as beautiful as ever. You'll probably look better." She trilled a laugh. "Our faces are the reflection of our experiences, and the more experiences we have, the more interesting we look."

Little girls Lucy, Cindy, and Bella rushed in, hugging Elly all at once. She hugged and kissed them in turn. Lucy whispered, "It's going to be fun, your living here. You'll be like a big sister."

"You're right." Elly giggled. "It will be fun."

Over tea, Sir William chuckled as his young daughters competed for Evan's attention. Quite the little gentleman, Evan loved the female adoration.

Katherine talked about rehearsals for THE TEMPEST. "Everyone's been terribly worried about Elly. It's remarkable. They all ask after her and send regards."

Elly sighed happily. "I have so many sweet notes and gifts in my room. "I have a lot of thank-you notes to write."

Katherine buttered a scone. "Wednesday morning, when you hadn't shown up for rehearsal, Jerry was livid. Then Isabelle called, hoping you were with us. Of course, no one knew where you were. Jerry was so disturbed, he dismissed us an hour early. Can you imagine Jeremy O'Connell cutting a rehearsal short?" she laughed. "He may have felt guilty for wanting to scold you."

Elly was terrified of asking, "Has anyone been doing my part?"

Katherine and Rory burst out laughing. Rory said, "Actually, Meg's been standing in."

119

Elly's mouth dropped open, picturing the buxom, over-painted bleached blond.

Katherine laughed so hard she could barely speak. "She's exactly the opposite of the lithe nymph Jerry has in his mind. Meg knows she's all wrong, but she's the only unpaid, unemployed female body available. Watching Prospero gaze up to what's supposed to be his higher consciousness, and then close his eyes in dismay, is terribly funny. Eventually, we have to engage a proper understudy for you. When are you coming back?"

"Tuesday."

Isabelle raised an eyebrow. "Only if the doctor says you're strong enough."

Katherine scowled. "Seriously, the sooner the better."

Miss Caldwell, Lord Richfield's typewriter, appeared with her shorthand book. Evan and the little girls went upstairs. Sir William, Rory, and Robert retired to the smoking room. Sam, Isabelle, Katherine, and Elly followed Miss Caldwell into the drawing room.

Katherine took Elly aside. "I know this is going to be hard for you. If you'd rather I didn't hear it, I won't stay."

Elly trembled. "Would you like to stay?"

Katherine shrugged. "I care about you. I'd like to know what happened."

Elly nodded. "Then, please stay." She looked at Sam. "The whole world will know in a few days, anyway."

Sam nodded. "At least a few weeks." His dark blue eyes were dancing and Elly smiled back.

Per Sam's design, he and Elly sat in cushioned chairs across from each other. Elly's ankle was propped up on a low stool. A pile of handkerchiefs sat next to her. Isabelle, Katherine, and Miss Caldwell sat behind, with strict orders not to make a sound.

With his good hand, Sam pushed the hair from his eyes, and positioned the plaster cast so it rested on the arm of the chair.

Elly grimaced. "Poor Sam. Does it hurt very much?"

"I don't know anymore, I'm used to it."

"I'm so sorry." Her throat tightened and she closed her eyes.

"You're not to blame, but go ahead and keep your eyes closed. Just relax. Now, in your own time... Tell me about last Wednesday morning."

For almost two hours, Sam calmly and insistently asked Elly questions. He sensed each time she left out a painful detail, and pushed her to squeeze out every possible memory of that frightful day.

Sitting behind Elly, Miss Caldwell scribbled madly, filling page after page in her shorthand book. Katherine and Isabelle sat tensely, listening to the ghastly story. Occasionally they reached forward to comfort Elly, and Sam shot them threatening looks, making them sit back. Katherine squirmed, hearing about Peg and Tommy, two actors she knew well and once cared about. She barely remembered a large, handsome supernumerary named Mick.

The story ended with Sir John's boot catching the hoop of Elly's skirt and pulling her out the window. Sam knew the rest.

When it was over, everyone was exhausted.

Sam smiled. "Well done, sweetheart." He winked an eye. "Thanks."

Elly sat very still. A shroud of heavy sadness had swallowed her completely.

Miss Caldwell stretched her cramped fingers. With half-closed eyes, she asked, "Mr. Smelling, how soon do you need this typed?"

"How soon can you do it? I know it's a lot."

"Sir William told me your work should take priority. I'll have most of it by tomorrow night."

"That would be great, thanks."

Miss Caldwell spoke to Elly. "You're a brave girl, Miss Fielding. Good night, M' Lady, Miss Stewart." She rubbed her eyes, opened the wide double doors, and left the room.

The clink of billiard balls sounded from the games room and Isabelle tilted her head. "Elly, your beaux are still here. Why don't you let them cheer you up?"

"No, thank you." Elly blew her nose. "After all this crying, I must look horrible."

Sam shook his head. "Vanity, vanity." He stood up and wobbled to keep his balance. "If you ladies will excuse me, I'm about to fall asleep. I'd better find a bed to do it in. Good night." He started down the hall.

Elly called after him, "I'm coming too." She lowered her sore ankle from the stool, and was careful not to make a face as she stepped on it. She had to convince Isabelle it didn't hurt.

Elly and Sam started up the stairs together. He stopped halfway and leaned against the railing. "You were great down there. Thanks."

121

She stared at the floor. "You're welcome."

"You went through a lot and you'll probably be feeling pretty sad for a while. It might be good if you went back down and had some company."

Elly sighed and shook her head. "You're sweet, but I need to be alone right now."

"I don't think that's a good idea."

"I'm terribly tired."

"I know you're tired." He winked. "Just give your guys a half-hour. They deserve it."

She rolled her eyes. "All right."

He led her to the games room and leaned in the doorway. "Fellas, I've got a present for you." He gently pushed her inside.

Rory and Robert dropped their billiard cues and raced to the door.

Half-asleep, Sam staggered back past the drawing room. Isabelle shovelled coal onto the fireplace. "Isabelle, surely you have servants enough to do that?" He tottered into the room.

She stirred the coals. "I thought you were going to sleep."

"Katherine and Evan gone home?"

"Hmm." She nodded. "She took some Opium Lettuce tea for Jerry, says he hasn't slept in days. Pull the bell, Sam, I want some cocoa. Join me?"

He laughed a giddy, sleepy laugh. "Cocoa? What a terribly comforting idea." He pulled the cord. Within moments a servant appeared.

The fire started to draw, and Isabelle sat on the sofa, watching the crackling coals. She slipped off her shoes, stretching her long legs.

He sat down next to her. "Isn't it unusual for Lady Richfield to be spending so many evenings at home?"

"It's totally absurd. I haven't been home this many nights in a row since my last confinement. What a bore that was. Even when the children are ill, I only nurse them through the worst. Then, I leave them to the nannies."

"You spend a lot more time with your children than most women -- of your class."

"I do. But they're so marvellous. I really don't understand women who go through all the horror of pregnancy and childbirth, only to ignore their children until they're seventeen. My mother kept us around her all the time. She's a truly great herbalist -- a marvellous teacher. She even kept Ned schooled at home until he was ten. You've never met my little brother, the dashing Sir Edward Hereford."

"He mailed Elly's letter from Paris."

She chuckled, "Yes."

"Sounds like a man with a sense of adventure."

"And a sense of humour. You'll like each other. He's coming for *THE TEMPEST*."

"Good. Does your family know Elly's becoming your ward?"

"Yes, I've written everyone."

"What do they think?"

"They're surprised."

A servant arrived with the cocoa. Sam tasted the hot, sweet creamy chocolate. "God, that's good."

Isabelle sipped her cocoa, sat back, and breathed deeply. "I'm surprised myself, about Elly." She smiled. "The only one who doesn't seem to be surprised is Bill. He said that he expected it." She shook her head. "I have no idea why that girl's become so important to me. No rational idea. She's darling, of course, but that doesn't account for it. The morning she was abducted, I called my solicitor and told him to draw up the papers. At the time, it seemed like the most logical thing in the world. I'm glad I did it, but it was certainly impulsive."

Sam leaned his cheek on the sofa, happily listening to her. Even the way she sipped cocoa was sweetly sensual. "So, you don't think Elly's your cousin?"

"I'd love that to be true, but how can we ever know?"

Sam's eyes were half-closed. "You've been like a crusader through all this. Absolutely fabulous."

"Elly's been fabulous." She shook her head. "Hearing her story just now, I'm not sure I could have gotten through an ordeal like that. Do you think she'll be all right?"

"She'll be fine. I left her in the games room with the guys." Sam's eyes squeezed shut and his face contorted with pain. He put his hand on his chest.

Isabelle sat forward, "What is it?"

His face relaxed and he took a deep breath. "It's gone... Comes and goes... The doctor's watching it." Tears filled her eyes and he smiled. "I'm flattered you care so much."

She let out a sigh. "I do care about you, a great deal." He raised an eyebrow and she looked away. "Sam, listen to me. I'm the luckiest woman I know. I..."

"We make our own luck."

"Perhaps, but I have everything a woman could want." She sipped her cocoa, her brows drawn together. "A friend once asked if Bill had ever been cruel to me. I found the question absurd. I can't imagine him being anything but gentle and kind. Elly was continually abused by men. Men who felt it was their right." She finished her cocoa and stood up. "I'm tired."

He watched her, hoping she would say more.

Finally, she half-whispered, "Sam, I adore you. Please, let's leave it at that. Get some sleep. If that pain persists, send for the doctor."

He nodded, then saluted with one finger. "Good night... little mother." She looked surprised and he smiled. "You're pregnant, aren't you?"

She smiled and went upstairs, the dark-blue of his eyes lingering in her mind.

Chapter Eighteen

Tuesday morning at 9:45, Sir William's driver delivered Elly to the stage door of His Majesty's Theatre. She ached all over, but lied and said she felt well. Dr Cummings believed her. Isabelle did not. She allowed Elly to go to rehearsal, but not return to Darry House with the other apprentices.

Elly promised she would sleep at Hamilton Place, be driven to the theatre each morning, and brought straight home afterwards. She loved the Richfields, but felt very guilty she was no longer poor. Going hungry had been horrible, but everyone at Mrs. Potter's Boarding House had been hungry. Darry House served proper meals, apprentices were no longer starving, but they still received no wages. Would they still like her, now that she lived in a mansion with servants?

The driver held the car door and Elly scurried inside the stage door. Quick as her sore ankle allowed, she greeted the stage-doorkeeper, and carefully climbed the stairs to the noisy rehearsal room. Actors and crew joked and studied their scripts. Lester, Todd, and Eddy Edwards set up platforms to approximate the stage set. Lester was the first to see Elly. He let out a war whoop, ran over, and lifted her off the ground. She loved it, but her shoulder hurt and she whimpered.

He quickly put her down. "Oh, I forgot you're injured. I'm so sorry."

She laughed, slowly rotating her sore shoulder. "Don't worry. I'm glad you're happy to see me."

"Happy?" He beamed. "I've never been so happy to see anyone in my entire life."

A dozen actors and crew surrounded her. They all talked at once.

"IF IT'S TOO LARGE, CUT IT DOWN OR MAKE A NEW ONE!" Jeremy O'Connell's voice boomed down the corridor. "I STILL DON'T CARE WHAT IT COSTS!" A hush fell over the hall. "I STILL WANT THAT BLOODY MOUNTAIN!"

Owen Richards put a hand over his eyes. "That's a perfect opening line for the week."

Ross Hamlin crossed himself and comically prayed, *"Kyrie eleison, Christe eleison…"*

Michael called out, "Katie, fix it!" and there was sniggering all around.

Rory closed his eyes. "Thank God Elly's back. Maybe she'll help his mood."

Ross scurried to Elly's side. "Aren't you lovely. I'm Ross."

Quick feminine footsteps announced Katherine Stewart's arrival. "Morning all." She saw Elly. "Welcome back dear, as you can see, nothing's changed." She hurried to the director's table and set out diagrams.

Jeremy's clipped step approached the door and a dozen actors held their breath. He charged in, made a sharp quarter turn in Elly's direction, and stared at her. She trembled. He had only engaged her because she was pretty. Now her face was bruised. Would he sack her?

He narrowed his eyes, walked up to her, put a hand under her chin, and studied her face.

She forced herself to look him in the eye.

His grimace relaxed. "Thank God you're safe." He kissed her forehead and walked to the table. "Act Two, Scene One ladies and gentlemen, if you please." A dozen actors scurried into place.

*

Throughout the week, Katherine and Eddy put Elly into scenes that had been staged while she was away. In two scenes she played Ariel's double, and she loved working with Michael. The rest of the time she was what Jeremy called, "a symbol for all that is beautiful on the island: Miranda's innocence, Prospero's magic, and all those things that must be left behind." She had to be in specific places, standing, sitting, or reclining in specific poses, on specific dialogue cues. Sometimes she was to freeze like stone. Other times she travelled around the stage. She learned quickly, moved with catlike grace, and seldom missed a cue.

Katherine directed Elly always to concentrate on Prospero. Elly loved watching Jeremy. She thought his every move was like poetry, and every word from his rich voice was like sweet music.

Jeremy gave her very few corrections and seemed to forget she was on the stage. Since he ignored her, she felt sure he was displeased. What was she doing wrong? If she knew, she could improve. Desperate to gain his approval, her eyes darted fearfully, and her body was tight as a rubber band.

During one long rehearsal, Eddy called a break. The actors scattered for a few minutes rest. Elly found a quiet spot on the stairs. Lester played a schoolboy joke. Sneaking behind her, he covered her eyes with his hands.

She screamed and he leapt back. "My God! I'm so sorry." He sat next to her clutching her flailing arms. "I'm sorry. It was only a joke."

"I know." Gasping for air, chest heaving, she forced herself to calm. "I know it was a joke. You didn't mean anything." She looked into his round face. His kind dark-eyes were frantic with worry. "Poor Lester, you'd never hurt me." She took a few deep breaths. "You've always been so kind." She pulled a handkerchief from her sleeve and blew her nose.

Lester's heart pounded. "You're so sweet. I don't know how anyone could ever have been unkind to you. I absolutely adore you. When you were poor, I thought, maybe... well someday, we might... you know... But, now you're an heiress, so..." He hung his head.

"No!" She violently shook her head. "I'm not, really. At least, I don't feel any different. I didn't earn my good fortune, and I don't come into any money until I'm twenty-one. I'm just the same as I always was."

He chuckled kindly. "You're not the same. We all read Sam Smelling, 'The Man With The Nose For News.' You might be related to Lady Richfield, and you've got money in your own right. I'm very happy for you. You deserve the best... it's just... well, you're not the only reason I'm going... It's just time I moved on." She looked confused, so he sighed sadly. "I'm leaving O'Connell's company."

"What do mean, you're leaving?" She felt weak.

"I've been offered a tour." Lester took his time. "You may not remember, but I've been an apprentice a full six months longer than Rory. Todd and I came at the same time."

"I do remember. You two should have been put on salary before Rory, and you've been overlooked. It's very unfair. I'm happy for Rory, but I wish..."

He sighed glumly, twisting his mouth. "...you also fancy Rory."

"I don't. Really, I don't. He can be sweet, of course..."

Eddy called down the stairs. "Come on, you lot. Break's over."

Lester helped Elly to her feet. She hugged him. "Will you write to me?"

He held her tight. "You're living in a mansion. Are you sure you want letters from a poor actor?"

"Oh, yes, very much."

He sighed happily. "Then, I'll write you every day."

When everyone was back inside the rehearsal hall, Eddy called, "Act One - Scene Two, please."

Elly was positioned on a precariously high, slanting platform. She was directed to stay perfectly still, and did her best to find a comfortable position. Jeremy's understudy played the scene first, so Jeremy could watch. Elly listened to Prospero tell Miranda the terrible story of their abduction.

The second time, Jeremy played the scene himself. This time, Shakespeare's words erupted with life. Elly not only saw Prospero and little Miranda dragged from their home and forced into "*...a rotten carcass of a boat...*," but her memory flashed to the "rotten carcass" of a freight train that had carried her to Yorkshire. She relived Mick grabbing her off the street and Tommy smothering her with chloroform.

Prospero's scene finally ended and she relaxed her pose. Her shoulder throbbed. She shook away frightening memories and fought back angry tears.

As opening night drew near, Jeremy held all-day rehearsals, finishing just in time to prepare for evening performances. Between matinee and evening shows, he checked the progress of his set and costume designers. After evening performances, he called the actors back again, rehearsing them until dawn. Like a comical mantra, "Katie, fix it!" became a catchword when anything went wrong. If a prop was out of place someone shouted, "Katie, fix it!" If a set piece fell over, a call of, "Katie, fix it!" made everyone laugh and broke the tension.

One night, the final curtain fell on the Scottish Play. The actors remained on stage waiting to be told what *TEMPEST* scenes Jeremy would rehearse. They all looked dog-tired, so he gave them an unexpected night off. Thrilled to have a full eleven hours rest before returning to the theatre, they raced away like children on a school holiday.

Jeremy had still not given Katherine her diamond ring. Tonight would be the night. He took Katherine and Evan up to his flat, and asked Max to prepare omelets and toast. Evan scampered upstairs.

Katherine slumped, exhausted, into the sofa. "That rascal's gone to finish the trifle. He won't be wanting any real food, after that."

Tired as he was, Jeremy paced in front of the fireplace, gathering courage. Finally ready, he perched next to Katherine. She reached a weary hand and stroked his cheek, prickly with a late day's growth of beard.

He kissed her palm. "Dearest Katie, you are remarkable, do you know that? I never expected you to be so marvellous at everything." He pressed her hand against his heart. "I almost feel superfluous. You could be mounting this entire production without me."

"Don't even think it. Whatever skills I have, I learned from you."

"Sometimes the student surpasses the teacher."

"Not in this case, darling. Not at all."

He kissed her passionately, drawing strength from her warm, shapely body. Gently holding his cheek against hers, he inhaled the subtle perfume in her hair. "Marry me, Katie. Our life is already so good. If we were married..."

"If we were married, I would still have to share you."

"You have *never* shared my affections. There is no one else I care for. You and Evan are everything to me."

Sighing, she gently pushed him away. "Not quite 'everything.'"

Starting to deny her words, he reached into his breast pocket and pulled out the diamond ring. He held her left hand and tried to slip the ring onto her finger.

Smiling with surprise, she took it from him, squinted, and studied the elegant design. "How simply marvellous, a genuine engagement ring." Chuckling happily, she ran it between her fingers, but did not put it on.

"Look what else I found." He held out a worn piece of paper.

She opened it and laughed. "How funny! This is our fake marriage license. I'd forgotten..." She read aloud, "*On this third day of December, in the year of our Lord eighteen- hundred-and-eighty...*" She squinted. "I can't read the year."

Jeremy nodded. "I had smeared it, intentionally."

"That's right, I remember." She read further, "*...at Christ Church, Bitby.*" She thought for a moment. "Where was Bitby?"

"It was where I lived in *The Bachelor's...*"

"*The Bachelor's Dilemma.* How could I have forgotten that silly play?" She chuckled and read further. "*...Service presided over by the Reverend Henry Plantagenet. Witnessed by Sir John Falstaff and Robin Hood...*" They both laughed until the upstairs' doorbell rang.

Jeremy scowled. "Who the devil is that, at this hour?"

"Clara's off. I better get it." Katherine started to stand.

Evan's nimble footsteps sounded overhead. Moments later Simon Camden's voice boomed down the stairs, "Hello, Evan. How's my boy?"

Jeremy shouted, "He's not *your* bloody boy." He whispered to Katherine, "You said he was in Edinburgh."

She whispered back, "I thought he was."

"Then, what is he doing here? He uses our flat as a free hotel, and your bed as the tryst de' jour." He folded the fake marriage license and slipped it in his pocket.

"Stop it, Jerry. Simon's not the Lothario he was in his youth."

"You're sure of that?"

She paused. "Well, he couldn't be. Could he? At his age? He's spent nearly every night with me."

Jeremy half-closed his eyes. "'Nearly every night,' and what about the days? In case you have forgotten, the male organ is on call twenty-four-hours running. Its appetites are equally strong at noon as at night. Do you actually think he wasn't with some hot-blooded Scots lassie last night?"

They turned as Simon's footsteps sounded on the stairs. Beaming with good humour, he marched into the room. "You won't believe my good luck. I've got the entire..." Seeing their gloomy expressions, he stopped short. "Is this a bad time?"

Jeremy glared. "Yes."

Katherine squeezed Jeremy's hand. "No, Simon dear. It's never a bad time. You know you're always welcome."

"What's your good luck, Uncle Simon?" Evan raced down the stairs. His face was smeared with jam and cream.

Since Evan was the only one smiling, Simon turned to him. "Well, I had planned on spending a full two weeks in Scotland, raising the final money for my tour, but one rich, kilted nobleman has found all the money at once, so I caught the first train back. You'd like to go to India, wouldn't you, Evan?"

Jeremy sprang up "No! He would not."

Frightened by the flash of anger, Evan backed away from Simon.

Katherine rubbed her eyes. "Jerry - Simon – Please! We're all very tired."

"Supper's ready." Max stood in the doorway. Behind him, on the elegantly set dinner table, three steaming omelets, a rack of toast and a pot of tea, gave off appetizing aromas.

Evan shuffled his feet. "I'm not very hungry, Mummy."

"I know. You've finished the trifle. Why don't you get ready for bed? I'll be up in a little while."

Evan glanced at the three adults positioned in an uneasy triangle. "Goodnight, Daddy." He hugged Jeremy, then his mother. "Good night, Uncle Simon." He took a few steps backwards, then sped up the stairs.

Simon watched them for another moment, gracefully spread his arms, pointed one foot, and bowed. "I shall be on my way, then."

Katherine stopped him. "No Simon, it's very late."

Jeremy huffed. "It is late. Why don't you stay upstairs? Clara's got the night off, but you can find everything you need. Katie will stay down here, with me."

Simon's eyes opened wide as Katherine muffled a smile and looked at the table. "There's an extra omelet."

"N' No, thanks, I... well, actually, I'm famished. Thanks." He went into the dining room.

Katherine started wearily after him and Jeremy took her in his arms. "Katie, please give me an answer." She stiffened, but he held her tight.

Relenting, she softened, hanging limp in his arms. "I'm hungry, Jerry. I can't think when I'm hungry."

"Oh, very well." Sighing deeply, he let her go and followed her into the dining room.

She sat at the table. She calmly slid the ring onto her finger, then placed a serviette in her lap, picked up her fork, and started to eat.

Chapter Nineteen

By now, most of England had read Sam Smelling's frightening newspaper report of Elly's abduction and the murder of Father Folen. The publicity was fantastic and advanced ticket sales for *THE TEMPEST* were astounding. Elly thought she might not get the sack, after all.

The next week, Isabelle allowed Elly to move back to Darry House. Elly was thrilled until she opened the door to her tiny room. She had forgotten it was so small. After the opulent rooms at the Hamilton Place mansion, it seemed almost shabby. There was just enough room for her to slide between the wardrobe and narrow bed with its cherry-red spread. The table and chair seemed child sized.

She pushed back the matching cherry-red drape, opened the window, and looked down onto the dark tree-lined street. A branch from a large tree reached toward the glass. She reached out and could almost touch it. If this were her old home, she might have tried to jump onto that limb. Sighing happily, she remembered she would never have to run away from anything, ever again. A frigid breeze blew in, so she quickly closed the window and the drape.

Exhausted after the day's rehearsal, she found a nightdress, blew out her candle, and sleepily crawled into bed. It was hard and small, nothing like her luxurious bed at Hamilton Place. Dim light from a street lamp shone through the thin red window curtain. She fluffed her small lumpy pillow and fell asleep.

She woke up hearing a strange noise. After a moment, she decided it was the tree branch scratching against her window. It hadn't done that before. The wind must have picked up. She turned over and closed her eyes. The scratching became louder. Wood creaked. The window opened. Her heart banged in her chest as the curtain moved aside.

A man crawled through. She opened her mouth to scream, and Mick whispered, "No' a word Autumn Lydy." A knife glimmered in his belt. She drew up her knees and pulled the covers tight around her. "You been 'avin' a righ' good time a' 'amilton Place. Couldn't get near y' there. Knew you'd be back 'ere sometime. I just 'ad to wait." He started toward her. She screamed as he fell on top of her. His weight was tremendous as he pulled off her bedclothes.

"Elly! Elly, wake up. My God!"

A match *hissed*. A candle lit. Lester stood next to her, his tattered nightshirt hanging off one shoulder. His black curly hair was mussed to one side.

Elly dripped with sweat. Her heart pounded. She leapt to the window and pulled back the curtain. The window was closed. Outside, the tree branch was perfectly still and nowhere near the glass. She put her hand over her mouth, forcing back tears. Lester put his candlestick on the table and took her in his arms. She clung to him. "I'm sorry. I'm so sorry."

"You had an awful dream."

"Yes. It was just another dream."

"Another? Do you have these often?"

"Just since… you know."

"That's awful. Does anyone know?"

"I used to have them a lot. Please don't tell anyone. Lady Richfield won't let me sleep here if she knows, and I want to stay, at least until the play opens." Her door was open. She looked out and was relieved to see the empty hall. She closed the door and sat on the bed. "I hope I didn't wake anyone else."

Lester sat next to her and put his arm around her. "I won't tell anyone, but this is terrible. Are you all right?"

She nodded. "Are you?"

"You scared me half to death." He kissed her cheek. They were quiet for a few minutes. "Are you going to be able to get back to sleep?"

"Sure, but not just yet. I'll stay up a bit."

"I'll stay with you." He yawned and shook himself awake.

"You're a dear, but you need your rest."

"So do you. Are you afraid to go back to sleep?"

"Yes." It came out with a sob.

"Will you have another dream?"

She shrugged.

He looked at the clock. "It's 3:00 o'clock. You can't stay awake all night. How's this, you get into bed and I'll sing you a lullaby?"

She giggled, "A lullaby?"

"Sure. Why are you laughing? Don't you think I know one, or don't you think I can sing?"

"You are so sweet."

"You just noticed? Come on, into bed." He held the covers and she crawled in. He tucked the covers around her and sat on the floor.

"Aren't you cold?"

"Freezing, so you'd better fall asleep fast. *Lullaby and good night, la, la ,la, la--, la, la, la!*"

She burst out laughing, "I thought you knew a lullaby."

His lower lip stuck out in a mock pout, then broke into a smile.

Elly rumpled his fuzzy hair. "You're so wonderful. Your smile could light up the planet. I loved my lullaby."

"Good. Now go to sleep." He kissed her forehead. "Promise you'll call, or knock, if you need anything? I'm right next door."

"I'll be fine, but yes, I promise."

He took his candle, left her room, and closed the door behind him.

Alone in the dark, she clenched her fists and beat her pillow.

*

The next afternoon, Elly knocked on Jeremy O'Connell's dressing-room door. He looked up, closed his book, and put down his pipe. Before she was properly inside, her words rushed out in a frightened whisper. "Will you help me? Please, can you help me? I don't know what's the matter with me. I hate myself."

"Tell me what has…"

"I'm afraid of everything. I cry all the time. I have horrid dreams. I don't think this has anything to do with acting, but can you help me?"

"Yes, I think I can. You have already helped me."

Her eyes widened. "What you mean? How can I possibly have helped you?"

He guided her into a chair, closed the door, and sat near her. "The intensity of your feelings taught me about Prospero's feelings, when he was abducted, especially with a small child to protect. I had been concentrating on the anger and the loss: Loss of control, position, comfort, companionship. I had given no consideration to the horror of the abduction itself. You brought that home to me, and I thank you."

"But you're not happy with my work. Please tell me what to do. I want to do well, but I don't know how."

"Everything you're doing is lovely. Why do you think I am not pleased? The only thing wrong is that you look frightened some of the time, and Prospero's Nymph is never frightened."

She clenched her fists. "I'm so sorry. I'll try harder."

134

"You are trying too hard as it is. You need to relax and trust that you are safe." She stared at him. He leaned in closer. "Do you understand what I'm saying?"

"I understand the words, but I don't know how…" She shook her head.

"Do you trust me?"

"Of course, sir, with my very life."

He caught his breath. "Well, I'm flattered. I also think that I deserve your trust. I think I've earned it. Can you trust that, whatever happens between now and the night this play opens… no matter if I howl like a banshee, or scold you, or insult you, or tear the scenery, or do any mad thing, that I respect you and care for you? If I am not pleased, I shall say so. If I say nothing, can you trust that you are doing well?"

She shrugged. "Yes, sir." Her palms were moist, her breathing fast and irregular.

Jeremy's eyes narrowed. "Katie told me about your abduction with many more details than Sam Smelling wrote in the paper. It was despicable. Beyond anything I can imagine. Being a journalist, Sam was interested in the facts, not your feelings."

"My feelings?"

"I know about Tommy and Mick attacking you on the street. Later, Mick tried to rape you. You kicked him and he struck you across the face. What were you feeling?"

She stared at the wall, her voice a monotone. "What was I feeling? How should I have been feeling?"

Jeremy's eyes bored into her, but he stayed silent, waiting for her to say more.

Every muscle in her body was tense. The emotional memory threatened to overpower her. Finally, she whispered, "I was afraid, terribly afraid."

"If Mick were here, now, what would you say to him?"

"I'd say that he's a… Forgive me, sir." She stood and started out of the room.

He blocked her way.

"Please, Mr. O'Connell…"

"Talk to me."

Her hands were fists at her sides. She thought she would explode, "Please let me go."

"You're a well brought up young lady, trained to repress you feelings. This is not the time to draw on that training. Talk to me, Damn it!"

"Please let me go, sir. I'm afraid of what I might say."

He took her hand, pulled her from the room, upstairs, and into the rehearsal hall. He slammed the door and glared at her. "Whatever you're afraid of saying, I order you to say it now."

She shook her head as her face contorted, "No, no, I can't," she sobbed. "It hurts too much."

"Do I have to make you?" He raised his hand as if to strike her, and she ran back against the wall. He scowled, raised his hands like claws, and menacingly moved towards her. "I'm Mick. Talk to me. Talk to Mick."

"Stop it, you bastard!"

He kept coming.

"You filthy piece of shit!" Her hands flew over her mouth.

He lunged, and she ran across the room.

"How dare you touch me? How dare you hurt me, or any woman, ever?" She took a deep breath.

Jeremy lurched at her.

"I hate you!" She tore back and forth like a caged tiger. "You should be dead. Peg should have driven that knife into your throat." Her eyes were wide with terror. "You're still out there somewhere. You can find me again. Oh, dear God!" She was shaking.

Jeremy nodded. "Good, now, what do you want to say to Peg?"

Tears welled in her eyes. "Why did you do it, Peg? Why? You told me you needed money. Surely there are other ways to get money." She shook her head, remembering, "First you lit a torch in my face… then you were kind to me on the stairs…"

"What stairs?"

"When I …bled on the stairs."

Jeremy's eyes were huge, "Peg was there?"

"Yes, and she was kind to me."

He shook his head in disbelief. "What do you want to say to your father?"

"I never knew my father." She paced the floor, breathing hard, pushing back her hair, tearing her fingernails. "I wanted to know my father, and my mother. My Uncle hated me because I stood between him and his brother's money. If I hadn't been an heiress, he might have thrown me into the workhouse, like Oliver Twist."

"Then, be grateful you had money. Talk to him."

"You bastard!" She leaned on the back of a chair, her knuckles white with rage. "You wanted me married to that fiend." She kneaded the chair back. "Now you'll hang. You'll hang like you deserve."

"What about John Garingham?"

"You're stinking dead. You fiend! You're rotting in the ground." She banged the chair on the floor. "Sons? You wanted sons? Another generation of bastards like you? You killed my father, and now you're dead. You're dead! I killed you!" She hurled the chair, crashing it against a wall. "I killed you..." She collapsed onto the floor sobbing. "...I killed you."

Jeremy slid onto the floor, next to her. "He was killed in a fall. No one killed him."

"I pushed him into the window. I knew the frame was weak. I wanted him to go through."

"Wanting a thing and causing it are two different things. You did not kill him." He clutched her arm. "Say it, 'I did not kill him, he fell.' Say it."

"I didn't..." She shook her head.

"Say it."

She whispered, "I didn't kill him... he fell."

"Now say this."

Exhausted, she shook her head.

"Say, 'I'm safe.' Say it. 'I'm safe.'"

Her throat was so constricted the words were barely audible. "I'm safe."

"Again."

"I'm safe."

"Again."

"I'm safe."

"Again."

She sat up, "All right... I'm bloody safe!"

He laughed. Slowly, she smiled back, through her tears.

"Now say this..."

"No more please." Exhausted, she leaned her hands against the floor.

Jeremy's face was inches from hers. His eyes bore into her. "Say, 'I'm surrounded by people who love me.'"

Stunned, she looked into his smiling eyes. Sunlight flooded through the windows, shining onto his smooth dark hair. The skirt of his magnificent silk dressing gown was covered with grit from the floor. His voice was like velvet. "'I'm surrounded by people who love me.' Say it."

She tried to speak, but the words stuck in her throat. She shook her head.

He gently lifted her hands from the floor, put them around his neck, and hugged her.

She leaned her face against his shoulder, whispering, "I'm surrounded by people who love me."

"Once more."

"I'm surrounded by people…" her voice caught, "…who love me."

They stayed still for a few moments, both breathing deeply. He gave her a tender squeeze and sat back. Slowly, he stood up, and helped her off the floor.

She gasped, "Your beautiful dressing gown. It's ruined."

He surveyed the damage. "I daresay Connie can clean it."

There was a knock on the door and the call-boy chirped, "Sorry, Mr. O'Connell, couldn't find you at 'alf hour. It's twenty-five minutes now, sir."

"Thanks Matt. I'm coming."

Chapter Twenty

The last days before the opening were exciting and hellish. Tempers were high and egos were frail. Everything seemed to go wrong and everyone blamed the person working under them: actors, scene-shifters, and even seamstresses. Jeremy O'Connell's temper stayed unusually even. Everyone credited his full-time nanny, Katherine Stewart. Occasional calls of, "Katie, fix it!" still brought a laugh and relieved tension.

Now, Jeremy played all the rehearsals himself. Katherine and Eric Bates sat out front taking notes. Post rehearsal note sessions went on for hours, and Elly could not imagine the principal actors remembering all the details.

There was a lot of debate over Elly's costumes. Her long copper hair flowed over various colours of pastel gauze. Underneath, she wore only a flesh-coloured body-stocking. Her arms and legs were bare and she appeared to be naked. She presented a picture so serenely sensual, just walking backstage brought gasps from both men and women. Jeremy loved the costumes, so Elly was content to wear them. When Eric Bates commented that the audience would be watching nothing but her, Jeremy redirected her to sit totally still during Prospero's scenes.

The technical dress rehearsal was a total disaster. Backdrops fell. Trapdoors stuck. Rigging tangled. The miniature boat sailed half-way across the sea, then flipped and hung suspended in the sky. Jeremy howled at Elly for being out of place when the entire set was stuck off stage. Worst was Jamie Jamison's gentle island mist, which gushed like volcanic ash. The entire stage level needed to be evacuated.

*

That same night, Jeremy's murderous Scottish King dazzled yet another audience. After the final curtain, he calmly wiped off his makeup, and mused about his adorable Katie. Not only had she just performed a brilliant Lady Macbeth, she had turned a horrific technical dress rehearsal into a bearable experience. He felt very calm as he meticulously cleaned every inch of his face and neck.

He gazed into his large wall-mirror and saw portions of the dimly lit backstage. A young man studied the rigging and set pieces. Only invited guests were allowed past the stage-doorkeeper, so this man had to be the friend of an actor or technician. Rather tall and pleasantly slender, Jeremy was struck by his easy assurance. His walk was graceful without being foppish or mannered. Jeremy had not shared a man's bed for months. The Scottish Play, Christmas parties, and rehearsals for THE TEMPEST had kept him too busy to miss pleasures of the flesh. This young man seemed extraordinary. Not knowing his sexual appetites, Jeremy still imagined taking him home, closing the door at the bottom of the staircase, and… NO!

His stomach cramped. His heart pounded. Beads of perspiration popped out on his forehead. There would be no door at the bottom of the stairs, or the top, ever again. This man was still beautiful and mystifying and Jeremy's lusty longings would carry on. Satisfying those longings could earn him a lifetime of loneliness and regret. The price was much too high. He watched the young man study a painted flat and run his fingers across the thick brush strokes.

Ah, hah! He was a painter. A painter? Christ! Jeremy closed his eyes and shook his head. He called, "Mr. Dennison, do come in."

Smiling delightfully, Robert Dennison loped gracefully into Jeremy's dressing room. "I was just thinking that if my exhibition failed, I might make a living as a scene painter. Your performance was extraordinary. The entire production was absolutely stunning." He pumped Jeremy's hand and sat down. "I hadn't seen Michael on stage since we were at school together. He's a marvellous actor and credits you with his skill. Elly spent an entire night talking about you. You have been very kind to her.

The day of opening night was eight exhausting hours of rehearsal followed by a two-hour dinner break. Food was brought in and people either stayed away with nervous stomachs, or gorged themselves for comfort. Everyone was running on pure adrenaline. Those who weren't pacing or chewing their nails were making bad jokes and clowning to relieve tension. Elly was dressed and ready well before half-hour.

*

At the Hamilton Place mansion, Sir William and Lady Richfield hosted a small pre-theatre party for two-dozen friends. Servants passed trays of champagne, and a generous buffet was set out in the dining room.

Simon Camden chatted-up a homely society dame. Never forgetting his workhouse roots, he never missed a chance to befriend someone with money. Believing that Katherine Stewart would wait until the last possible moment, finally agree to marry him and join his tour, he had cast everyone but a leading lady. He heard Isabelle's laugh, turned and watched her tease her brother. He mused to himself. "They're two-peas-in-a-pod. Ned's as handsome as his sister is beautiful. How will he react to Elly?" Smiling wistfully, Simon remembered that delicious, half-naked girl on the floor, backstage. He wanted her again, this time in a bed.

Isabelle had fashioned Sam Smelling a one-armed tailcoat, fitting over the cast on his arm. He came downstairs and she straightened his tie. "You look delightful Sam, just like the *Swan Prince* in the fairy tale."

Sam grimaced. "That's not funny. This thing is heavy. It's hot and itches like crazy. I want it taken off."

"I know you do, darling, but the doctor insists it stays on." She pointed to the dining room. "Ned and Robert are at the buffet. Let them get you some food."

Scowling, Sam joined the other young men. Both were taller than he, and he was annoyed he had to look up. He was even more annoyed to hear them speaking French. He waited a moment, then asked, "Do you guys provide a translator? You seem to know each other."

Robert laughed. "I'm sorry, Sam. I thought you knew Lord Hereford."

Sam's right arm was in the cast, so he offered his left hand, "It's good to meet you, finally."

Sir Edward Hereford smiled and shook with his left hand. "It's my pleasure Mr. Smelling, and the name's Ned. You're newspaper pieces about my young cousin were riveting."

Sam smiled at the easy, left-handed gesture. "Thanks Ned, and my name's Sam. You and Isabelle look like twins."

Ned bowed. "Thank you. I think she's far better looking than I am, and she is five years older."

"Do you believe Elly is your cousin?"

"Isabelle would like me to. I've never met the girl. I just posted her letter from Paris." He nodded at Robert. "I haven't seen this scoundrel since he left Paris. What was it, a year ago?"

Robert sighed, "It seems like a lifetime ago."

"Rob is one of many fine artists I had the privilege of assisting, financially."

Sam looked over the food. "So, Rob, how are the commissions coming?"

Robert bowed. "I'm delighted to report I have enough work to keep me busy for two years. Fully half come from friends of Lady Richfield. Ned's delightful sister has unlimited friends yearning to be immortalized. It will take me at least that long to repay my father's debts, but as a schoolmaster, I might have been indentured for life. Most important is that my mother will never lose her house."

Sam hung his head, "Guys, I'm starving and can't get to any of that food." Both men rushed to serve him, and Sam laughed, "Thanks, I love the attention. So Ned, if you're twenty-eight and single, you must be on the front page of this season's Stud Book."

Ned groaned, "This, and every season."

Robert took two glasses of champagne from a passing waiter and nearly dropped them. "Is there really such a thing as a human Stud Book? I thought it was a bad joke."

Ned started to give Sam a plate of food, saw that he couldn't eat standing up, and carried the plate to a small table. "Oh, it's real all right, and a damn nuisance. I have no desire to marry anytime soon, so I spend part of the year in Paris, and another part in Scotland. I own woollen mills and raise horses there. The remainder, I live here, or at my mother's home in Kent."

Robert handed Sam a glass. He took a sip, set it down, picked up his fork, and dove into steaming chunks of lobster. "Your mother's estate is legally yours?"

"Legally, of course. When father died, I inherited. Since the estate came from mother's family, I'll always consider it hers."

Robert applauded. "You're a man who believes women should own property, unlike Elly's miserable uncle."

Ned rolled his eyes. "Of course they should own property. Women should also be able to vote, copyright their work, earn as good a wage as a man..." He held up his hands. "Please don't get me started on women's suffrage. I was a huge supporter, even before my sister took up the cause."

A quarter hour later, the butler sounded a small gong. It was time to leave for the theatre. Sir William donned an evening cape and escorted his guests outside.

Chapter Twenty-One

"Fifteen minutes!"

The riggers cursed as they made last minute adjustments to the miniature boat.

"Beginners! Full company on-stage!"

Two-dozen actors rushed downstairs. Jeremy O'Connell gathered them into a tight circle.

Elly stood with all the actors, stretching their right arms until their fingers touched, like spokes of a human wheel. The energy was centered by Jeremy, darkly-bearded, with a mane of thick grey wig-hair hanging down his back. His eyes were painted to look huge and fierce. His cheeks were sunken. His smile was sincere.

He placed his right hand atop all the others. "This is a play about love and wonder, ladies and gentleman. So, now, everyone together: Love and Wonder." Two-dozen actors cheered, "LOVE AND WONDER!" then broke apart, laughing with excitement.

The orchestra finished its pre-show music and received polite applause. As the houselights dimmed, excited chatter rose from the audience in boxes and stalls. When the lights went out, the theatre was silent. A sudden symbol crash, blaring horns, screeching violins and cellos accompanied the curtain rising on a howling tempest. Far in the distance, a fierce storm pitched a great ship as if it were a toy. The miniature boat behaved perfectly, tossing and turning in the cardboard sea. Backstage, the riggers sighed with relief. The small boat disappeared as the bow of a life-sized boat appeared on-stage, thrashing in the merciless waves. The sailors cried out in fear.

The next scene began as beautiful Miranda pleaded with her father to stop the tempest. Prospero told her the frightful story of their abduction, their drifting at sea and eventual landing on this magical island. A perfectly controlled blanket of white mist covered the floor, as a fantastic nymph appeared to grow, wild and naked, out of a magical marsh.

From their box seats, Isabelle gasped and clutched her husband's hand. Sir William's eyes were like saucers. Sam Smelling grinned, and Simon Camden raised an eyebrow. Robert Dennison's heart pounded.

Isabelle's brother gazed at the vision. He whispered, "Is that Elly Fielding?"

Isabelle nodded.

"She's beautiful. I hope she's not my cousin."

Isabelle chuckled silently.

*

On-stage, Elly concentrated on Prospero. She wanted nothing more in life than to react to his every move, his every inflection, every blink of his eye. She trusted her emotions to be honest reflections of his every need.

*

Three hours later, Prospero faced the audience for his final monologue. Alone in his beautiful island paradise, with only a slender nymph for company, he crooned his last words:

"...As your crimes would pardon'd be,
Let your indulgence set me free."

He joyously strode downstage-right. At the last moment, he turned back, waving a final farewell to all the beauty he was leaving behind. His lovely nymph, swathed in mossy-green, seemed to grow out of the hillside. She reached her arm in a bittersweet goodbye. They held each other's gaze for a moment. Smiling triumphantly, Jeremy winked at her. This was totally unexpected. He had never winked in rehearsal. A happy laugh bubbled from her lips. Taking a deep breath, Jeremy raised his head and walked off-stage.

Realizing she had lost Prospero forever, the nymph's arm reached further. Tears ran down her cheeks. The curtain lowered and a cheer rose from the audience.

Jeremy strode into the wings and the open arms of Katherine Stewart. Actors raced past them, onto the stage for their curtain calls. Jeremy held Katherine tight. His heart pounded. In a single move, he pleaded, "Don't leave me, Katie," turned and walked to the edge of the wing, ready for his bow.

Elly sped offstage as scene-shifters moved set pieces, allowing enough space for the entire cast to stand on-stage for their curtain call.

Michael grabbed her arm. "I'd never seen you cry like that. It was fantastic." They watched the dozen other supernumeraries standing in a single line upstage. Evan was in his cabin-boy costume. He smiled at Elly

144

as the curtain rose. Michael gave Elly a shove and she joined a second row of ten minor players. Rory, Lester, Todd and other actors bowed together. One-by-one, the principal actors, Donald, Michael, Owen, Sandra, and Ross walked to center-stage, took their bows, and stepped back to form a third line. Last was Jeremy O'Connell.

Katherine watched proudly as the audience rose to their feet. Jeremy accepted their applause, raising his arms and smiling at the top balcony. He bowed alone, then stepped back and joined hands for a company bow. The curtain fell and immediately rose again. After ten curtain calls, Jeremy stepped forward and quieted the crowd.

"Ladies and Gentlemen, your kindness overwhelms. We humble servants of the bard, are eternally grateful for his genius and your generosity." He took hands with his leading actors for a final bow. After that, the curtain was still. The curtain leg had not broken. All was well. The backstage lights came on, and a jubilant cheer rose from the cast and crew.

The next Sunday, the matinee curtain fell on *THE TEMPEST* and everyone hurried away for a well-deserved, two nights off. Jeremy quickly wiped off his makeup, while his dresser pulled the soiled costume off his sweaty body. He dashed to the men's washroom, and joined other sweaty actors scrubbing themselves with brown soap and tepid water. When he returned, the dresser was ready with a spanking new, very elegant morning suit.

Actors and crew raced by, wishing each other a good holiday. Jeremy hurried to Katherine's dressing-room and was greeted by Evan, looking like his exact miniature. From the sheen on their beautiful top hats, elegant cutaway coats, and boldly striped trousers, they could have been an illustration in *Gentleman's Weekly*.

Eager as schoolboys at Christmas, they found Katherine taking special care, pinning up her hair. She looked stunning in an ivory-coloured suit. Jeremy's heart swelled with pride. In a few hours, they would finally be a real family. After twenty years of playacting, Jeremy felt like he was becoming an adult.

Evan pouted, "Please, Mummy. Can't I stay with you?"

Jeremy pulled him close, whispering, "No. Sorry, old chum. Right after the ceremony, Max is taking you home. I want my bride to myself on my honeymoon." He was delighted to see Katherine blush. "Look Evan, I've kept my part of the bargain and we're travelling in one of those smelly motorcars you're so curious about. We'll only be gone the two nights."

Evan dropped his narrow shoulders and shrugged with defeat.

Jeremy glanced out the door. "I think everyone's gone, Katie, don't be long. We'll wait for you outside." They hurried out the stage door, past the stage-doorkeeper sitting on the steps eating a sandwich.

Bright sunshine and puffy clouds dotted the bright blue sky. It was a lovely day for a drive. Evan hurried to the hired motorcar and talked with the uniformed driver. Max, thrilled to be the best man, relaxed in the back seat.

"Hello Jerry. My, my... Aren't you looking the real toff. Doing something special are we?" Jeremy's heart stopped as Simon Camden ambled toward him. His ship was supposed to have sailed for India the day before.

Jeremy tried to sound civil. "Actually, we're in a bit of a hurry - off for a weekend in the country."

"Ah well, I'm off to India tomorrow. Just thought I'd pop 'round to say, 'Goodbye.'"

"You'd best get along then. We're off in a minute."

"Right-i-o." He hurried inside.

Jeremy cursed silently, gestured for Max and Evan to stay put, shrugged an apology to the stage-doorkeeper, and slipped back inside. He listened outside Katherine's open door.

She saw Simon and said, "Good God!"

"My timing's impeccable." Simon sounded apologetic.

"I thought you'd already sailed..."

"Change of plans. My character man broke a leg, so I can't leave until the morning. I've engaged Tommy Quinn to take his place."

Jeremy nearly fell over and it sounded as if Katherine did the same. She gasped, "You're joking."

"Amazingly, I'm not." There was a creak of wood and Jeremy guessed Simon had helped himself to a chair. "Tommy calls himself Leo Thomas now. My tour manager put out an urgent call for character actors and we were overrun by has-beens and elderly novices. Tommy showed up in an excellent disguise. I knew it was a wig and makeup, but didn't guess who was underneath until I saw the missing tooth."

"But, he's wanted for murder." Katherine voice was shrill. "A man was stabbed in his pub."

"I know, I know, but he explained that he didn't even know the blokes involved. I see no reason to disbelieve him. Whatever Tommy is, he's not violent -- and he's a good actor -- and I need one."

"What about kidnapping Elly?"

"He says Peg proposed that escapade. He never touched Elly. That Mick person battered her. Elly's father was arrested before he could pay them off, so Tommy showed up at my casting-call broke and desperate. Tomorrow we sail for India, and he won't skip out on me this time. I'm withholding sixty percent of his wages until closing night."

"Where has Peg gone?"

"I've no idea. Since the lassie sets houses on fire, I have no desire for her company. Oh, I saw Jerry downstairs. Says you're off for a weekend in the country. Nice suit... I didn't think you liked white. You always said it soils too easily."

Katherine was silent.

Finally Simon asked, "Do I have any straws left?"

Jeremy almost laughed out loud.

Katherine sighed, "Haven't I given you more than enough?"

"There's no such thing as enough, when two people are in love." Simon's melodramatic inflection made Jeremy flinch.

"Are we 'in love'? I did love you. For years, I loved you -- since I was a child. You were my dancing Prince -- my everything. I left my family for you. I followed you to London and you deserted me after one night. Even then, I waited for your letters as though they were golden."

"They weren't gold?"

"More like sawdust."

"Oooo! That hurt..." There was silence, then, "I'm sorry... am I ever sorry." Another pause, then, "So, Jerry's won after all." There was more silence, but now Jeremy's heart raced happily.

When Simon spoke again, he sounded like his old, randy self. "Oh well. In a month's time, I'll be on the jewelled continent. Who knows what delights India will bring?" Katherine laughed and Simon asked, "May I still write to you?"

"Oh yes, please do."

There was silence. Jeremy thought he heard a kiss. Simon said, "I love you both. I wish you well. Of course, if you change your mind..." She laughed again, and Jeremy tiptoed back outside to the car.

Evan and Max were in the back seat playing cards. Jeremy flipped open his pocket watch, then panicked slightly as Katherine, a vision in soft bridal white, arrived outside holding hands with Simon. He kissed her cheek, waved to Jeremy and walked away. Jeremy took a deep breath, and stepped back so the driver could open the car door.

The stage-doorkeeper looked relieved. He could finally go home. Standing stiffly, he stretched, tossed his sandwich leavings into the top of a nearly full dustbin, and went to lock the stage-door. Before his key was in the lock, Evan leapt from the car, seized the sandwich scraps, and raced back into the empty theatre.

"Evan! To hell with the sodding cats," Jeremy shouted after him, "We don't have time... Bloody hell!"

He shrugged another apology and raced inside to see Evan tear up four flights of stairs. Following him was useless, so Jeremy walked onto the stage and watched him scamper across the catwalk, high overhead. The only light filtered in from windows in the stairwells, but the day was bright. Evan balanced himself with the rope handrail and set down the sandwich. He turned to go, but stopped as a dark shadow moved over him.

A large workman walked onto the middle of the platform. "Scraps for the cats, is it?"

Jeremy called, "Sorry friend, but the theatre's closing for two nights. Whatever your business, it will have to wait until Tuesday."

Evan started to hop off the catwalk, when the man flung him over one shoulder like a sack of flour. Evan screamed and squirmed to get free. The man clutched the rope handrail, shouting, "Hold still you li'le bugger, or I'll toss y' over."

Evan stopped struggling, hung limp, and stared down at Jeremy.

Jeremy stared back, helpless and terrified.

The man looked pleased with himself. "So, Mr. O'Connell, I said I'd be back in this theatre and 'ere I am. Just came for some clothes an' some money, but now I got your li'le prince. 'e gets everything 'e wants, does this one. Just like that cow, Elly Fielding." He bounced Evan on his shoulder, and Evan screamed.

Jeremy's heart pounded. Sweat streamed down the back of his neck. He yelled, "Let the boy go. Please, let him go and we'll pretend this never happened. Just take whatever you want and go."

Even at that distance, Jeremy could see the man shake his head and grin. "I was just a lowly actor. Did a damn good job for y', and y' tossed me out like a side o' rotten beef."

Jeremy's heart stopped. It was Mick Tanner, the butcher's assistant and would-be actor who had nearly murdered Elly. Powerful enough to haul beef carcasses, Mick stood thirty feet in the air, holding Evan like a calf going to slaughter.

A thin, dark-haired boy appeared at the side of the catwalk. "Come on, Mick. I got what we come fer. Let's go."

Mick stood his ground.

"Put 'im down. 'e ain't done nothin'. The money were just where 'e always left it. We go' plenty, an' we dan want any more trouble."

Jeremy caught his breath. The boy was Peg McCarthy. Mick swung his free arm, effortlessly tossed Peg against the rope handrail, but lost his balance at the same time. Forced to clutch both rope handrails for support, he released his grip on Evan. Jeremy watched helplessly as Evan's small body slid from the massive shoulders and crashed down onto the narrow walkway. Peg snatched Evan aside, as Mick slipped off the catwalk and fell to the stage, three stories below. Jeremy turned away as Mick's head split open, like a melon hit with a spade.

Two hours later, Evan was the happiest boy in London. He did not care that he had been seconds from certain death. He raced between police officers and the press, vividly describing the crime scene over-and-over. He was a sudden celebrity.

There was no sign of Peg McCarthy and Jeremy secretly hoped she had escaped. Whatever the girl had done in the past, today she saved Evan's life. He would always be grateful. Eric Bates's office had been burgled and a substantial amount of money stolen. That seemed like poetic justice. The wages Hilda Bates withheld from starving actors had finally been paid, at least in part.

After Jeremy told his story to the police and the press, he and Katherine retreated to chairs in the wings. When the draped body of Mick Tanner was carried past, they were still in shock.

Jeremy clutched her hands begging, "Promise you'll never leave me."

She closed her eyes. "I promise."

"And I promise, from this minute, to be a proper husband to you." She shook her head, but he plowed on. "I've engaged carpenters to take down those doors between the floors, tear out the wall to my guest room, and make a proper bedroom we will share every night."

"You can't..."

"From now on, if I see a beautiful man, I will look at him, but I will not act on my feelings -- never again. I will never risk losing you."

She shook her head and laughed softly.

He stuttered, "W... Well... I will try..."

Her laughter grew. Embarrassed, he laughed with her, "...very hard." They laughed harder and louder, until they had tears in their eyes.

Their wedding was delayed only a few hours. Evan, the ring bearer, held a velvet cushion with two real gold rings, not the cheap gold-coloured metal Katherine had worn for so long. That evening, Jeremy and Katherine shared their wedding night in a country inn, truly as Mr. and Mrs. Jeremy O'Connell.

The marriage license was signed by a real vicar and not the Reverend Henry Plantagenet. The real witnesses were Max and the vicar's wife, not Sir John Falstaff and Robin Hood.

Chapter Twenty-Two

Young actors Elly, Rory, Meg, and Todd stood on the train platform, hugging their dear friend Lester Reid. He was dressed in his one shabby suit, holding a cloth bag with his few belongings.

Elly wiped tears from her eyes. "I'm so happy for you darling, but I'll miss you terribly."

Rory playfully socked his arm. "Well, I'm jealous. You'll be seeing the country, playing leading roles, while I'm still here playing servants and solders."

Lester chuckled. "I can't believe they're trusting me with Falstaff. I've got five other roles to learn at the same time. I already know Bottom, but I've never heard of these new plays. They run five plays in rep'. We've never done more than three, and that was with weeks of rehearsal. I may get no rehearsal at all, just…"

Sobbing, Todd threw his long wiry arms around Lester. "Don't go!"

Lester patted his back. "There, there, Toddy. Buck up old thing. You survived before you met me. You'll do well again."

Elly gently pulled Todd off Lester. Todd fell into her arms and she held him tight.

Meg sniffed, "You promised to write, but it don't sound like you'll 'ave the time."

"I'll let you know I arrived safely. After that, you're right. I may not be able to write for a while. I'll miss you all, so much. We've lived through a lot together. I'll never forget those horrid years at Mrs. Potter's. No lodgings will ever feel shabby after that."

The train whistle blew and Rory opened a door on a third class carriage.

Lester held his arms wide, and everyone joined in a group hug. He stared at Elly and tears streamed down his face. Without another word, he boarded the carriage, closed the door, opened the window, and leaned out. The train whistle blew. Steam from the engine billowed past, as huge iron wheels groaned slowly, moving the massive locomotive and passenger cars behind it. They all waved and threw kisses. Quickly, the train was out of sight.

Rory wiped his eyes with the palm of his hand. "Anyone for a pint. I'm buying."

Meg sniffed, and blotted her already smeared eyes. Black makeup smudged down her cheeks. "Thanks ever so', Rory, but I've go' a bloke waitin'."

Todd giggled and wiped his teary eyes on his sleeve. "I got a bloke waitin' too."

Everyone laughed as Meg and Todd walked toward the underground.

Rory looked at Elly, but she shook her head. "I promised Isabelle I'd spend these two days off at Hamilton Place. Why don't you come, at least for tea?"

Rory chuckled, "Of course I'll come." He took her arm and turned towards the underground.

She gently pulled him toward a row of hansom cabs. "Isabelle insists I only travel by car or carriage. I don't know why she frets so."

They were quickly at Hamilton Place. They left the carriage and walked towards the front door.

A tall young man ran out from beside the stoop. "Miss Roundtree?"

Elly froze at the sound of her old name. Rory moved protectively in front of her.

The man wore a cloth cap and wrinkled short coat. He held a small note pad in one hand and a pencil stub in the other. His face was bright with anticipation. "Are you Elisa Roundtree?"

Rory demanded, "What business is it of yours?"

"I'm a reporter for the *Daily Mail*. I was just hoping to get Miss Roundtree's feelings about the upcoming trial."

Elly was ashen. "What trial?"

"Anthony Roundtree's going on trial for murder."

Rory pulled Elly up the steps.

"Surely you know he's being tried for the murder of a priest?"

Rory rang the bell, whispering, "Come on, someone answer the damn door."

"You know, you'll be called as a witness."

Horrified, Elly turned back.

"Oi, you there!" A policeman ran toward the reporter, waving his nightstick. "I told you lot to vacate…"

The door opened and Rory pushed Elly inside.

Smythe slammed the door. "Sorry, Miss, sir. Sir William called the police. This morning the street was swarming with them, newspapermen that is." He took their coats. "Sir William's in his study with the solicitor, Mr. Foxhall. He arrived shortly after the story broke."

"What story?" Elly's eyes were like saucers.

Rory grabbed her hand and they hurried to Sir William's study.

Sir William and Mr. Foxhall sprang to their feet. Sir William hurried from behind his large mahogany desk. "Thank God!" He solemnly shook Rory's hand, hugged Elly, and led her to an upholstered leather sofa. He turned back to Rory. "Was there any trouble at the theatre?"

"No, sir." Rory turned to the solicitor. "How do you do, Mr. Foxhall?"

The solicitor shook Rory's hand. "Better, now that you've delivered the young lady safely home."

Elly asked, "Please Sir William, what's happening?"

"Things are moving faster than we expected, that's all." He resumed his seat behind the desk.

Rory sat beside Elly, and Foxhall return to his chair.

Elly sat stiffly. "What things? My uncle has been in jail for weeks, waiting for the circuit judge. Chief-Inspector Hayes said he would be swiftly hung, so what was that reporter talking about? Why will there be a trial?" Elly stared at Foxhall's round face, thin grey hair, and intense eyes.

He nervously curled his moustache. "My dear, the coroner's inquest determined that the Reverend Laurence Folen was murdered by a bullet from Anthony Roundtree's revolver. Your uncle will be tried in a court of law to determine if it was murder, or manslaughter."

She shook her head. "Forgive me, sir. I don't know what that means."

"Your uncle committed murder, if he shot the priest on purpose. He committed manslaughter, if he shot the priest by accident. We know your uncle was holding the loaded revolver, but we do not know if he actually intended to shoot the priest."

"What's the difference? Father Folen died."

"There is no difference to the unfortunate victim. There will be a great deal of difference to the accused, your uncle."

The room was deathly silent as Elly digested this information.

Foxhall continued. "If your uncle is found guilty of manslaughter, he will go to prison at hard labour for a good many years. Gentlemen of his social class, unused to physical labour, usually die in prison before their terms are up."

Elly caught her breath.

"If he is found guilty of murder, he will be hanged." Foxhall shrugged. "Which would, in all likelihood, be the kinder punishment."

Rory and Sir William tensely waited for Foxhall to present his next piece of information.

The solicitor looked toward heaven, took a few deep breaths, and sat back in his chair.

Elly perched on the edge of her chair, wishing this was another nightmare and she could wake up.

Foxhall spoke softly. "My dear, another man died that night."

Elly blurted out, "Sir John Garingham. Everyone knows that."

"Now, now." He held up a hand. "Calm yourself, please."

Elly glanced at the other men. Both sat like stone.

"Miss Roundtree?"

She turned back to Foxhall. "Yes, sir."

Determined to keep himself calm, he presented the next information very slowly. "The coroner determined that Sir John died by misadventure. He leaned against a window, which only hours before, had been loosened by Sam Smelling. I am still not clear why Mr. Smelling did that."

Much to their surprise, Elly smiled. "I told Sam that when I was little, I used to run away by climbing out the windows and down the trellis. My father nailed the windows shut, to keep me in. Sam thought I might need to run away again, and pulled out the nails."

Foxhall smiled appreciatively. "Very resourceful." His piercing eyes bore into her. "So, when Sir John was startled by the gunshot, he lurched back, pushed through the loose glass, and fell to his death."

Elly froze.

Foxhall glared at her. "That is what happened. Is it not?"

She pursed her lips. Colour drained from her face.

"Miss Roundtree." He soothed, "That is the way it happened. Is it not?"

"I, I don't…" She looked frantically to the other men. Neither spoke, but both seemed to beg for her compliance. She whispered, "Yes, sir."

All three men released their breath.

She stared around the room like a cornered rabbit. Her voice was breathless. "Sir John was leaning against a loose window. He was startled by the gunshot. He lurched back and fell through the glass. I ran to help him." Perspiration slid down the back of her neck. "I was too late. He fell. As I reached for him, his boot flew up, caught the hoop of my skirt, and pulled me out the window, after him. I was thrown against the side of the house." She caught her breath. "My hoop caught in the trellis and I couldn't get loose. Sam Smelling climbed up to help me, and the trellis broke. We both fell to the ground." Her head spun as she gasped for breath. "Sam was terribly injured, I was injured…" finding a handkerchief, she clenched her jaw and blew her nose.

The three men visibly relaxed.

Foxhall smiled and sighed deeply. "That was excellent. This short bit of dialogue may be the most important of your life."

"I'm an actress," she wiped her eyes. "I'll remember my lines."

"See that you do."

End of Book 3

About the Author

Christina Britton Conroy is a classically trained singer and actor who has toured the globe singing operas, operettas, and musicals, as well as being a Certified Music Therapist and Licensed Creative Arts Therapist. She has published several books, and *Truth and Beauty* marks the third in the four-book *His Majesty's Theatre* series.

If you enjoyed *Truth and Beauty please share your thoughts on Amazon by leaving a review.*

For more free and discounted eBooks every week, sign up to the Endeavour Press newsletter.

Follow us on Twitter and Instagram.

Made in the USA
Middletown, DE
21 July 2018